For Denise, Oona and Simone

.

The World
And All That It
Implies

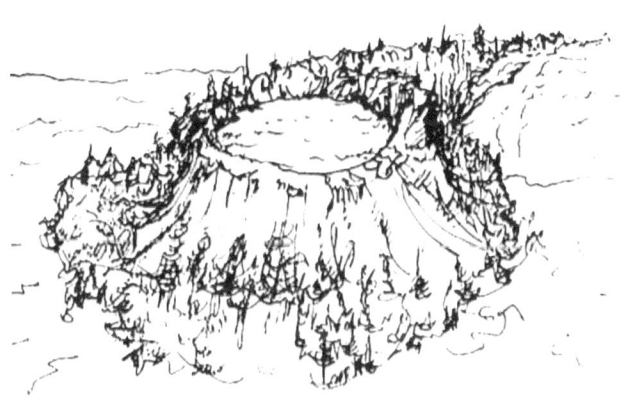

Philip Stephen Drury

To him a happy Lot befals
That hath a Ship, and prosp'rous Gales.

Table of Contents

Chapter 1   **The Imagining**

Sitting in the waiting room of the neurologist's office it is instantly apparent to me the I prefer blank walls to cheap art. My impatience with such décor is veiled by an apathetic countenance – eyes cast downward, following the worn trail in the carpet. Yes, I prefer white walls most definitely.

Staring intently at a blank white surface one can conjure up numerous spectacles and images. Bright, flashing dots of red and green, subtle nuances of gray and blue washes that dissolve and emerge again. Before long the wall is adrift with rhythmic swells and sways, no longer a flat two-dimensional surface but a living, organic entity of expanse and infinite mystery. The art, on the other hand, is dead and insulting – even when it is a poster copy of a true work of art – it hangs lifeless like a mounted Moosehead.

Still more to the point, in this age of technological wonder, everyone in the room is consumed by their phone/computer/mobile distraction gadget/fixation/cancer agent##. Why bother with art?

Better to save money and forego the embarrassing aesthetics. I fix my stare on the corner where two white planes meet and imagine the space to be convex instead of concave. Then I imagine it as it is, concave, then switched back again to convex. This optical gamesmanship is quite easy to do provided you do not pay attention to the plane of the ceiling or the plane of the floor. Without these two optical cues the space is capable of being understood both ways. Before long the two viewpoints meld into one and I am transfixed by a volume of space that has become spherical, undulating in and out, all around. All that was solid was now fluid and a peculiar blueness enveloped the space.

It was here that I first got the notion to sail the open sea and soon an idealistic juggernaut of a plan was hatched, ill- conceived, yet full of promise. Gazing at the white planes continually morphing forward then backward, they soon formed an opening - the doors of perception shall we say - to a quantum dimension, a simple but inspired visualization. It was a way out of the world of itinerant zombies and into a world of possibilities. Not a temporary world of daydreams or pipe-dreams but a truly new world, an Amazon beyond 2-day shipping. An uncharted haven where "I am that I am" actually makes sense. Religion and its discontents aside, I felt compelled to strike out, take the hero's journey and find myself - or some facsimile therein.

My plan was to sail aimlessly on the choppy blue without a map or GPS until, at some distant cross-section of longitude and latitude, I would inevitably find myself. It was critical that I distinguished finding from seeking. I knew who I was, but I somehow lost my sense of self and let him disappear into the fog of social subservience. So, I set sail and, surprisingly, found myself before the following dawn. Realizing what a bore I had been and still was, I then changed course and decided to forget myself altogether. I returned to land to revise and recalibrate my new world order.

Chapter 2 **The Realization**

Our world is a cacophony of alarming sounds - beeps, buzzes, dings and dongs - that remind us, wake us, and prevent us from all sorts of things. Every morning is the same annoying routine of waking, dressing, pissing and aching mitigated ever so slightly by a labor-intensive cappuccino, and shuffling around on the grid of glazed tiles until everything has been collected for the start of the day. With a jerking motion, I cast a number of pills into my mouth and invariably get one stuck in my esophagus, at which point I push on my throat with my thumb in order to dislodge the pill and allow it to resume its journey to the stomach, intestinal tract, bloodstream and ultimately, the brain. I am by nature an irritable person (aka depressed) and so, having consulted with my doctor and entertained numerous drugs, I have found a balance that keeps me me, or at least the me I would like to be, more specifically, the me I think I should be. Therefore, for years Damitol has been my habitual morning friend, confidant, pill that never lets me down nor quite lifts me up but certainly does not disappoint, this being somewhat of a given, as the whole purpose of Damitol is to stave off disappointment.

* * * * * * * * *

Damitol - Generic Name: Patascholderin (pat-a-sholda-rin)

BEFORE USING THIS MEDICATION: WARNING: This medication may increase the risk of suicidal thoughts or actions in children, teenagers, and young adults. However, life and certain other mental problems may also increase the risk of suicide. **DO NOT TAKE THIS MEDICATION** IF you are taking or have taken a monoamine oxidase inhibitor or MAO (not the chairman, although this would be good advice as well), a selective serotonin reuptake inhibitor or SSRI. Do not use this medicine if you are allergic to any ingredient in this medicine. **THIS MEDICINE MAY CAUSE** drowsiness, dizziness, lightheadedness, fainting or blurred vision; alcohol, hot weather, exercise, or fever may increase these effects.

DO NOT DRIVE OR PERFORM OTHER POSSIBLY UNSAFE TASKS **such as, singing, reciting poetry, or operating heavy-handed philosophical notions.** IF YOUR DOCTOR **tells you to stop taking this medication you will have to wait for at least 5 days before taking certain other medications.** IF YOUR DOCTOR **immediately prescribes new medication then** CHANGE YOUR DOCTOR **or sue him if** YOUR LAWYER thinks you have a case.

 POSSIBLE SIDE EFFECTS:

SIDE EFFECTS that may occur while taking this medication include constipation, decreased sexual desire or ability (hence, suicidal thoughts), diarrhea, dizziness, drowsiness, dry mouth, headache, increased sweating, loss of appetite, nausea, sore throat, tiredness, trouble sleeping, vomiting, or weakness. **CONTACT YOUR DOCTOR IMMEDIATELY** if you experience bizarre behavior (this may be hard to distinguish from regular behavior) bloody or black, tarry stools (yek!); blurred vision; confusion; dark urine; excessive sweating; fast or irregular heartbeat; fever or chills; hallucinations(depending on type); loss of coordination(provided you have coordination); new or worsening agitation; anxiety; panic attacks; aggressiveness, impulsiveness, irritability, hostility, restlessness, or inability to sit still; red, swollen, or blistered, or peeling skin; ringinginthe ears; stomach pain, tremor, trouble urinating, unusual bruising or bleeding(see domestic abuse); severe mood changes(PMS?); vomit that looks like coffee grounds (what?), yellowing of the skin or eyes. Symptoms of an allergic reaction include rash, hives, itching, difficulty breathing, tightness in the chest; or swelling of the mouth, face, lips, or tongue; unusual hoarseness. This is not a complete list of all possible side effects that may occur. If you have questions, contact your health care provider. Several weeks, months, years, decades may pass before your symptoms improve.

* * * * * * * * * *

Health is that nebulous thing that does not become a subject of conversation until one no longer has it. Generally, this occurs around middle age when one is showing signs of entropy - fatigue, arthritis, aches and pains of all varieties - and life becomes a series of doctor appointments and drugs. I take more drugs now than I ever did as a young budding scientist experimenting with hallucinogenic curiosities, mind altering Mephisto's and hydroponic horticultures. In fact, one can track age by the buildup of prescriptions followed by the installation of bigger medicine cabinets which you convince yourself is really for the benefit of a bigger mirror.

I am in the process of building an entire room for my medications. It is, I tell myself, shelving for books but I don't have any books as I no longer read them. The extensive information that accompanies each of my prescriptions keeps me busy enough plus I find the subject matter intriguing, somewhere between fiction and non-fiction.

Eventually, one gets quite bored with drugs. I no longer think "I need a new drug" so much as , I need a new neurosis or ailment. I watch TV, read magazine inserts and three-page drug advertisements in order to keep abreast of the latest disorder and accompanied symptoms.

Erectile Dis-function heads the charts, but I don't suffer from that and I hope not to in the future. The ads do tempt one with the idea of a four-hour erection. What possibilities lay in the arena of a four-hour erection? How many women could one exhaust? Will drugs of this sort turn us into philanderers and rapists? Does the penis expand and grow larger due to these extended periods of extension? I study the information in small print - it reads like a modernist poem - but I do not find answers to any of these questions.

Anti-depressants are a close second. I have tried most of them and have settled on one that is effective yet silent. But this is a disorder I already subscribe to so it gets listed under the bored category.

I am intrigued by restless leg syndrome, or RLS, monograms being the *in* thing for just about everything but especially suited to disorders. I have experienced RLS before and have attributed it to having allowed myself caffeine after 5pm. Now it is a respectable syndrome, in its own right, and I can take a drug for it if I so choose. Nervous shaking or maintaining a steady rhythmic beat with one's leg while sitting in a waiting room or riding on the bus does not qualify as RLS but you could probably convince your doctor to prescribe the drug anyway. Personally, I don't see the problem in allowing RLS to proliferate in society at large. I envision multitudes of people shaking, jiggling and stamping their legs at all hours of the day, in all places. Perhaps it would eventually be understood as a cultural thing, a kind of dance that perpetuates exuberance and well-being.

Overactive bladder is an up and coming competitor. It is a

legitimate problem but not all that appealing. I do think it merits attention with respect to health but as an agent for better health perhaps; the idea being that the constant trips to the bathroom requires you to get up out of your chair or off the couch and move quickly to a relief station thereby providing the sufferer with a workout routine that maintains a healthy heart rate and toned leg muscles.

Sleeping Disorders enter the game with a sweeping strategy. What could be better than taking a pill to fall asleep when you want, wake up when you want and greet the day refreshed and brimming with energy. The ads are as obvious as a shoe with laces. Relatively young, thin, attractive, well- proportioned women snuggling into their beds, dropping off to sleep with butterflies fluttering or sexy female angels guiding them to never-never land. These subjects do not seem the type for sleep disorder. They look as though they have been sleeping soundly for their entire life. Where, one asks, are the irritated elderly men and women with drawn faces and dark eyes sitting at the breakfast tables with disgusted looks and horrible posture? No -no - no, none of these disorders are desirable or tasteful. I need one with panache, substance, esoteric charm - one that is unique yet benign.

Turret's Syndrome, although not all that unique, does offer

esoteric charm and panache. What could be better than to have a legitimate excuse for gesticulating and swearing at people wherever and whenever one wants? I tend to do that already but I don't have the advantage of proclaiming it a disorder. Instead I am viewed as a foul-mouthed, ill-tempered person when, in truth, I am a compassionate well-meaning soul who happens to dislike people and society in general.

What I mean is, as a whole, I want the best for society. A decent living wage, healthy and affordable food, a reasonably effective health care system and free alcohol.

The problem is that whenever I leave my apartment absurdity reigns and people begin to unnerve me within minutes. Just walking along the street is a challenge, what with all the baby carriages (as big as SUV's in some cases), the dog walkers (really?) or the zombie phone carriers, is it any wonder that one is annoyed?

Today I decided to leave my serene, low-lit apartment in order to pick up some groceries for dinner. I opened the door and I was immediately assaulted by the Woop Woop of a police car and a fast-paced parent rushing by with a screaming baby nestled in its Sport Utility Stroller.

WTF?

I stand there for a moment and wonder if this is a good idea after all. Maybe there is something to eat up there that I had neglected to see. A moment of semi-muffled activity ensues and I regain my resolve to head to the market. Having retrieved the essential items (four in all) I engage in the hellacious activity of deciding which checkout lane to use. I peruse a few and come upon one where the person ahead of me has one item left to purchase. Yes! I enter the lane. A split second later, my mind tells me that I have fucked up. I should know better than to take advantage of what looks like a promising opportunity because, in all of my experience as a New Yorker, it is these promising opportunities that, through some kind of metro monkey business, decay quickly into frustrating ordeals.

The lovely lady ahead of me, it seems, has brought with her a stack of coupons for the piles of cat food cans in the cart (these were cruelly blocked by her big ffff ass....) and so I was unaware and so was unaware that this was a setup. The cashier was a plain and gently person barely capable of keeping her hair back from her face while scanning the coupons at a pace that would make a sloth envious.

I stand and look around while trying to hide the fact that I am swearing like a motherfucker under my breath. Another person enters the lane and begins unloading items onto the space left behind mine. I glance politely at her and turn my head so that I can get one more swear in.

The situation progresses like glacial ice recedes and then, finally, it is my turn to purchase my items.

Beep, beep, beep, beep....scan the card....done. Wow, how hard was that?

Having survived the checkout debacle, I walk towards the exit but find that I cannot exit because (big fff ass....) is at the doorway looking at the announcement board (why the fuck is the announcement board right by the exit door) and blocking my way. I step back and turn my head towards the checkout counter which I had just escaped from and monitor the current events there. All is moving well and good. Nice, I think to myself. This is just fine and everything is as it should be. I take a deep breath and wish that I had donned a suicide vest before leaving the apartment.

The woosh of the automatic door shifts me back to reality and I see that my lady friend has moved on. I exit the market and take a left while the coupon lady exits to the right. After a few steps, I stop. I cannot help but turn around and look back to see her waddling down the sidewalk with her bags of cat food. I scream out "Hey, coupon lady, I hope your fucking cat dies!"

She, of course, hears nothing and suddenly I am looking like some crazed fucker screaming at nothing and no one in particular, which although common in the city, is not something I was hoping to achieve when I left the apartment.

I manage an uneventful ramble back to my apartment, put away the groceries and recline in my chair. I am in a thoroughly poor mood now and stare over at the computer then lean back my head and close my eyes. Moments later a blaring blast of deafening noise jolts me upright. Nothing to be alarmed about though, it is just my neighbors from down the street riding by on their Harley Hell Raisers. I am lucky enough to be living on the same block as the Hell's Angels motorcycle consortium, which monitors decibel levels in the area and moves to annihilate any silence that may be lingering there. I have not figured out what they have against quietude, except that they must be suffering from a severe case of Decibel Addiction.

I have encountered a similar species in the countryside an hour's drive outside of the city.

Miles of gorgeous, winding roads follow the lead of old canals that parallel the Delaware river, a drive deemed one of the most picaresque on the East coast. Yet, here as well, one has to contend with volumes of calamitous Harley hobos who are compelled to raise the decibel readings to exceedingly noxious levels. How enjoyable can it be to rattle one's brains and assault one's (and everyone else's) eardrums while riding along these roads? Why can't they wear headphones that blast personalized audio artillery into their heads? This would offer far more possibilities for them and mitigate the annoyance for everyone else. Obviously, it has more to do with fucking with public space rather than satisfying their personal needs.

Aahh, but who am I to criticize. This is a democracy and we (all of us) have every right to be ignorant, loud, and otherwise unfit for communal living.

Evolution#ringing own dinner bell#mutant gene#melting pot.

Chapter 3   **The Reflection**

I was not always this way. Back in my youth, like most youthful minds, I was hopeful and enthusiastic about all that lay ahead. The world was full of possibilities. I was full of possibilities. Coke was "The Real Thing" and Andy Warhol was the Einstein of the Art World, due more so to his hair than anything else.

I was fresh out of college, full of intellectual and philosophical despair, and ready to make my mark as an architect. I moved to Manhattan and within months I was making my mark as a professional hack, working for wealthy real estate magnates looking for innovative ideas for their investments. Initially, I proposed several ideas involving sustainable energy and ways to retrofit their apartment buildings with renewable energy sources, solar for one, creating a viable alternative to the cement, energy sink holes that dominated the city. This particular idea, went over with about as much enthusiasm as an honest accountant.

So, I smartened up and introduced another idea having to do with the water towers that sat atop most buildings. I had devised an ingenious method for cleansing the water in these tanks of all chlorine and leaving the water cleaner and healthier than it was before. This idea was also greeted with cold indifference, similar to the indifference one might have towards non-alcoholic beer. I was a quick study though and realized that if I was going to make my mark, any mark at all, I would have to get smarter yet. As the saying goes "the third time's a charm" and my third attempt was warmly received and I was coldly annoyed but glad to have something to do that would keep my talents sharp.

Forget cleaning the water in the water towers, who cares, the important thing is that there is water. But what about all of those unsightly tanks littering the rooftops and spoiling the skyline? This could certainly be addressed with more creativity and imagination. I sketched out the idea and wrote up what could be described as a manifesto and pitched the idea to my employers. The idea was to transform these archaic cisterns into modern architecture. Build an edifice around them in the style of the best modern architects of our day and thereby create a kind of museum of modern architecture perched high above the maddening crowd, situated closer to the heavens where these great masters belonged.

Bingo!

They loved the idea and I couldn't make drawings fast enough. First was an enclosure built to mimic Frank Lloyd Wright's renowned Guggenheim Museum. Instead of cement (the weight would have made it prohibitive for a rooftop) I formed the structure out of polystyrene coated over the outside with structolite and painted white - it was a beauty. Next? Why the Guggenheim Bilbao a la Frank Gehry, of course (Franks and Guggenheims dovetailing nicely), with its soaring planes of shining Titanium. I was able to exploit some connections in the architecture community and scrounge up enough scraps left over from Bilbao and other Gehry projects and this supplied all that I needed for the tower construction. On I went conjuring up the likes of Louis Kahn, Eero Saarinen, Alvar Alto, Peter Eichenman (the most fun), etc. I copied them all. I was the rapper of architects - "R-K-Tect sampl'in the dogs of modern cribs."

It wasn't just fun and games either. There were many

challenging aspects to this work. Experimenting with suitable materials and combinations of materials, building in a cost-effective manner, completing projects on time and within budget (none of these guys did that), all while remaining true to the ideals of each of my mentors. I made a fuck of a lot of money too. All of these real estate moguls were silly with competiveness, each one wanting to outdo and outspend the other. I pit all of them against one another in a way that would have made Picasso proud. By the time the project was complete, the tower cost nearly as much as the original building.

This was all moving along in a most splendid fashion until the fucking Tech bubble burst. Suddenly, it was over.

Chapter 4   **The Awakening**

I wasn't fully awake when I heard a faint kind of licking, lapping sound. Quiet Finley, I said, assuming it was the dog who had a habit of licking his paw with a loud, sloppy, slapping sound that one cannot avoid being disturbed by. Like licking up a huge dollop of peanut butter and schlopping and schlooping it against the palette of the mouth until it finally works its way down the esophagus. Anyway, this was the sound I was hearing. Finley is licking my face, I thought.

Finley, NO!

I cannot summon the energy to say more than that. Usually this is effective enough but the licking does not stop. I soon realized that not only was I hearing this peculiar sound but I was also being jostled back and forth in perfect synch with it. I braced myself and tried to gather the strength to direct a more effective command.

FINLEY STOP IT! and with that my eyes open, not completely but enough to take in light and blueness, true blue, a blue not filtered through trees or polarized by a windshield, an all-encompassing, infinite blue that startles me. What am I seeing and why so much of it? The lapping sound is there too. I lift my hand to my eyes, my arm seems heavy as a leg of lamb, two legs of lamb in fact, or so it seems, and it is wet.

My guess is that the dog has been licking my arm for quite some time, and it is heavy and waterlogged now. I attempt to lift my head as well, but this is impossible, my head will not budge. It feels as though it is strapped down, but it couldn't be. Why would it be? No, I simply have to concentrate more and focus my energy on the muscles of my neck. It is as though I am a newborn again without control of my head, no strength, or more precisely, no muscles prepared for, or capable of, lifting my head. Not only this but I realize now that I do not know where my head is much less how to move it. I lay here, too weak to move my head and too tired to care. I do not know where I am, but my hand is shading my eyes and I am grateful for the relief it gives.

I no longer feel the licking, but that lapping sound is still there. The dog must be licking his paw instead of my arm. Was I dreaming before coming to this semi-conscious state? I cannot recall anything, at least, not directly. I did not know how long I had been asleep, or if I had been asleep. So, where was I before all this licking? I must have been sleeping but probably not very long because I am so very tired still and feel that the only thing to do now is go back to sleep if sleeping was what I was doing before all of this confusion set in. I must be getting sick, I think to myself as I slip into a reflective fog. Sickness often starts with a debilitating fatigue and one wants only to sleep and wake up well again.

- *Come on Joe, just one little one? Your money is no good here Ray*
- *Aw Joe, just one little taste, what's one little drink gonna do huh?*
- *Alright one, and then on your way, right?*
- *Yeah, yeah, come on, quick*

I am awake again, I guess? I can hear that licking, lapping sound again. Damn that dog! Why won't he stop. OK, I know I was sleeping just then because I was dreaming of an old black and white movie. I always dream in black and white movies, sometimes movies I haven't seen but have heard about or read about many times. I'm not sure how long I had been sleeping but it seemed to me that it must be around cocktail hour.

Ah yes, a drink would be very nice.

But what exactly is this place? I am completely drenched and everything around me is floating in a good foot or so of water. Wind is whipping it into a froth and I cannot open my eyes long enough to see what's going on. Lightning crackles loud and sharp, a huge branch has fallen close beside me. I feel the need to hold onto something but why?

I feel as though the earth is tilting and I am about to slide off into the abyss. Another tremendous gust and - shit - I am going to slide off into the abyss. I manage to grab hold of something, a rope I think, but I soon lose hold of it and go rolling back and over myself smashing into something solid which keeps me from sliding any further. Severe pain now between the shoulder blades and everything is escalating to a genuine panic - panic stricken I am, nothing less.

Everything is swaying and sloshing and I am using all of what strength I have to stay still, not move, not do anything but remain still and secure. I am huddled up against something, I do not know what, but it is keeping me anchored and safe for now. Meanwhile, there is water everywhere and rain pouring down with a relentless wind. The swaying and sloshing grows more intense. Suddenly I feel myself rising, everything rising, like being sucked up into the sky and then I am falling fast, dropping so rapidly there is no question that I am going to smash through whatever is below me. All of the fluids and organs in my body go weightless pushing at areas I never felt before.

As this feeling begins to ease I sense that I am about to hit. Instinctively, I tuck my head between my knees and make like a ball, squeezing so tight everything aches. My mind explodes with fear and I let out a scream, a deep- seated primal scream from some ancient pit in my gut and pass out.

- *Hey old man, how bad can it get? I asked you a question. Do you hear me?*
- *Well, first storm we ever had here was back in '35, wind whipped up a big wave and sent it bust'in right over*

Madacumba Key...eight hundred people washed out to sea.

- How far away was that from here?

- Oh...a few miles

- I don't believe it, eight hundred guys gett'in washed out to sea. You're a liar. Nobody would live here after a thing like that.

- Make a big wave, send it crashing down on us, destroy all of us if need be but punish him.

- Shut up old man! I'm warning you - Shut up!

- Hear me, hear me...

* * * * * * * * * *

Silence now, except for the slopping sound. I open my eyes but then close them immediately; it is too painful to keep them open. They are cold and raw from the wind and rain - Wait - cold and raw? No, more like burning and tender. I sense my whole face, in particular, my nose, broiling with pain. I know that it is very bright because of the intensity of the light that penetrates through my eyelids. There are flashes and dots everywhere as I rub my eyes and try to open them again. I sit up, (this takes several attempts) and slowly, ever so slowly lift my eyelids. BLUE - nothing but BLUE - no foreground, background no figure ground relationship at all - just BLUE. How can I be nowhere like this? Perhaps I am asleep, but this is in color. I am also very wet. How did I get so wet? The dog is gone but the lapping sound is still there. I am astonished to find that I am floating in water, ocean to be exact - the middle of the ocean! Well, not the middle of the ocean surely, not the middle of anywhere, it is simply somewhere and nowhere which is a kind of middle I guess.

I am definitely waking up now, but still cannot get my brain to click and make sense of things. I am straining to gain some sort of consciousness but still only a fog of being that accounts for nothing, except pain. Every part of me aches and I cannot understand where I am or what has happened. All I see is blue sky and blue ocean - I think my eyes are blue - and a feeling of space like I have never experienced before.

Nothing to see in any direction. It seems as though everything is, at once, up close and very far away. It is a strange sensation to have such an expanse of space before me. There is nothing to reach for, no place to move to.

Nothing to do but gaze out into the blue enigma. I sit here and stare for a long while, and as I do, certain images begin to form in my mind - a boat... a sail... a sailboat.

My sailboat!

I was sailing wasn't I? My dream wasn't a dream, it was a reality. I am beginning to get it. Synapses are firing again and I am starting to get a sense of what had or might have happened. The storm, the winds, the swell, the boat on its side and then upright - then on its other side and everything tossed about, floating and sloshing all around me. Then this calm awakening.

I can focus and see again. I Look around and try to make sense of things. I pat the surface to both sides of me, it is smooth and hard. It seems that I am afloat on top of the bottom of my boat. Yes, capsized. The boat must have capsized. I am stranded out in the ocean aboard a capsized boat. I have read about events such as this but never, never did I think......

I feel a rush of confusion along with a desire to scream, so I scream FUUUUUUUUUUUUUUUUUUUUUUUUUUUUUUUUUCK!!

Damn, this is really something. All emotions are rising up at once, my head is spinning like an isotope, all of my atoms careening about creating a conscious me again. I feel energized but confused. I try and calm myself and think. I need to call someone, a friend preferably, and then help. I have got to tell them where I am, where

I should be. Wait a minute, slow down. How the hell do I know where I am. I still do not remember where I was going in the first place. Where the hell is my cell phone anyway? I look around and search my pockets.

Nothing.

Fuck, this is great. I am, God knows where, and have nothing but the clothes on my back. How am I going to do anything with respect to being rescued? I can wave my arms and scream but I am nothing but a stranded, tiny dot on a huge ocean - not even a needle in a haystack. I take a deep breath and then another – then several more.

You know what, screw this. There is time for all that rescue shit later. I mean really, like I have to worry about being rescued. Hell, in this day and age, one has to work at getting lost. Severing ties with the World Wide Web, co-workers, friends, and the IRS. No easy task.

I need to let this play out more, make it epic, you know, right to the brink of disaster. Well, maybe the disaster part is extreme but, damn it, I have a chance here for something truly spectacular and I have got to take advantage of it. I only hope that I am not rescued too soon as this would abruptly end all possibilities for a life altering experience, not to mention the lucrative book deal, appearance on major talk shows and the obligatory movie rights.

I am battling technology more than this wide-open sea bullshit. I am lucky if I have more than a day or two to myself. I am sure that the Coast Guard is already on my trail, already making plans for a heroic helicopter rescue which will be scheduled to coincide with the evening news.

The Coast Guard consists of some 40,000 or so uniformed people, all of whom are eager to perform, to fly in with all of their state of the art gear and determination. I can see the proud smiles and the thumbs up execution of all of the operations they have been trained to do.

Shit, I don't want to be some poster boy for Coast Guard efficiency.

But what are my options?

Best case scenario? Being discovered by a fishing boat or cargo ship in 3 to 4 days ,maybe a week, actually, a month at least. A week or less barely counts as news at all. This has to be a genuinely newsworthy event. But, more than likely, I will be GPS'd with pinpoint accuracy and airlifted to safety before I even get a taste of an adventurous struggle with death.

Then what? I will be bantered about on radio and television. Oprah will exploit me for a full hour trying, without the least success, to identify with my plight and engage the audience with

OH's and WOW's and When We Come Backs. I hope to God my cell phone is resting soundly on the ocean floor.

I could beat them all to it though. Yes, I could play the game. Starting now - get the edge on it all. Hell, that's it! An account of the whole event while it's still happening, not after the fact, when I am back home safe from the what if's, beleaguered by the fog of memory, dogged by the wave of publicity (I know, cheap pun). I have got to write it down so that it has immediacy, like a heart attack or something. Every reader will be there with me, thinking and feeling as I am right now, virtual reality man!

OK, first off, let's take stock. I have been sleeping. That is the first thing I know to be true. It seems my boat is capsized. I am still alive. How or why I am still alive is simply dumb luck as far as I can tell. I don't recall sleeping through the night, but I know I must have. I remember preparing the sails for the overnight, the setting Sun, glorious on the horizon to the west and everything around me reflecting a warm, peach colored glow. So, unless I had been knocked harder than I think, I am pretty sure I slept through the night and awoke in the late afternoon of the following day. Dusk is once again approaching.

That's it? Barely 24 hours at sea?

I need more time - more shit to happen. Maybe a shark or two -

Nah - everyone has a shark story these days. For now, I should probably retrieve what I can from the cabin and get myself set up for the evening. I don't remember what I had stowed on board. I know that I bought a lot of emergency items (did I know something?). Some of them I bought because I thought they might be useful and some simply because they were cool looking, state of the art gadgets. I bought a relatively inexpensive ashtray made of bronze. It was round and flat, kind of like a worn pebble, with a lid that opens out into two semi-circle flaps that function as cigarette holders. I don't smoke, I bought it for its aesthetics. I figured I would find some use for it eventually. The most expensive item I purchased was the short-wave radio expressly for this type of situation. Well, not exactly this type of situation since a capsized boat with all my essentials trapped under water and an expensive radio, no doubt, shorted out was not what I had in mind. I suppose all or most of that stuff is history now but good stuff to itemize for the insurance. As for the items I need immediately, water is priority one.

Dehydration is not pretty, even if I am out here for only one or two more days I will need water. You can survive for about a month without food but only a few days without water. I know I have a case of bottled water on the boat, stored in the cabinet at the bottom of the stairs. There are some cheese and meats in the mini fridge and,

I am fairly certain, I stashed some canned goods in the cabinet as well. Question is, can I get down under the boat and salvage some of these things. This is a dangerous proposition. I could get trapped and drown or the last remaining air pockets could fill with water and sink the boat, pulling me down with it.

I do not like the idea of drowning. It is said to be one of the more peaceful ways to die (how the hell do they know) but I am terrified of drowning. I imagine the frantic writhing and kicking, the bulging eyes, the face like a blowfish and feeling like your lungs are about to explode. But your lungs do not explode. The body, starving for oxygen, goes into reflex mode and breathes in heavily, filling the lungs with water. Still short of oxygen the brain shuts down, you lose consciousness and die shortly thereafter. Charming, what could be more peaceful than that, eh? No, drowning is not my preferred way to leave this world.

I always thought sleeping pills would do nicely. Most people say that they would like to die in their sleep (after a good long life of course) so that death seems more like a dream that continues on forever - nice.

Imagine. Your dream state is sustained while your conscious and your physical state ceases altogether. For all you know, you are still dreaming. Does the dream change course and take you towards some miraculous vision as Dante would have Beatrice do? Life (your dream) ends as mysteriously and as effortlessly as it began.

We, none of us, remember our birth just as we do not remember our death. Suddenly we are somewhere else and we realize it later, or not at all. There is darkness and then there is light. There you are, a slithering, slimy being just learning to breath and no idea where you were just a few seconds before. Death is just the reverse. There is light and then darkness but one is no longer able to reflect on what existed just seconds before.

- Yah, you've got it alright, your system has already absorbed it.

- Are you sure Doc, are you absolutely certain? Couldn't there be some mistake?
- There it is. The toxin is actually luminous in the dark. No, there's no doubt about it Bigelow
- Give it to me straight Doc

- Well, a number of things are involved. The systemic condition of the individual, the amount consumed.
- Yes?

- You won't feel too badly for a while. Then it will happen

suddenly, a day, two days, a week at most.

- A day? Two Days?

- There's nothing that can be done now. I'll arrange for your admission to the hospital immediately of course. I'll have to notify the police, this is a case for homicide.

- Homicide?

- I don't think you fully understand Bigelow, you've been murdered.

All the talk about death must have tired me out. I have no recollection of nodding off, but my dream says otherwise.

Anyway, reflecting on death is not the best use of my time. I have got to prepare to dive under the boat and salvage what I can. This is not particularly appealing to me, at this time. I am safe and secure on top of the boat. Jumping off into the water, swimming up inside the cabin - holding my breath the whole time while looking through cabinets and grabbing whatever I can carry back up to the surface - seems like a ridiculous thing to do.

Am I nuts?

The Coast Guard is starting to sound pretty good to me. Wait, it hasn't even been 24 hours and I am already thinking of bailing?

Man, what a sorry, pathetic creature. How hard can this be? I will just dive down under the boat. A reconnaissance dive. Have a look at what I am up against, what it is I need to do and how I need to do it. First, I will practice holding my breath. Two minutes should be enough to get me under the boat and assess the situation.

Okay, hheeehpp ... hold it ...hold it ....main thing is, keep your mind off what is happening, don't think about the fact that you are holding your breath, don't think about what your lungs and chest are experiencing. Stay calm, look around, be comfortable with the situation and don't ... hhaaaaaah ... Shit. I don't think that was even one minute.

Huh, okay we're just going to have to work at this. Build up strength and stamina, work up to it. Heck, it's my first go at this. What did I think was going to happen? Just because I don't smoke did I expect holding my breath for long periods of time would be easy?

Let's try this again.

Here goes ... heeeeeeeeehp ... yah alright, much more relaxed now. Look at the beautiful sparkle on the water, like fireflies flashing on and off. The sun is so hot. I am getting burned pretty bad out here. The water will soon cool me down, refresh and reinvigorate me.

... hhoooooh ..huhhh... Good, much better, easily a minute and a half this time around. I think I can count it out without making myself too anxious ... One hundred eleven, one hundred twelve, one ... hheeehp ... hundred thirteen...

The pain is unbearable, it builds in the chest and throat until all you can think about is opening your mouth to inspire a boatload of air, a most satisfying breath ...hhooooh... Shit! My heart is punching me. I am going to die before I get started. I'll just catch my breath for a minute or two.

I will have to do this dive naked, I don't want to be plagued with soggy clothes for the remainder of the day and besides, clothes will only add weight and drag.

* * * * * * * * * *

That will have to do for now. Three dives and I have exhausted what little energy I had and am satisfied with five bottles of water and some cheese. This will certainly suffice and tomorrow I will do a few more dives. I also managed to cut away a large piece of the sail which I use now as a kind of poncho. Later I will salvage some wood and whatever else I can muster, in order to construct some sort of tent. The sun is merciless out here and I will more than likely burn to death if I cannot find a way to shield myself from these merciless light waves.

No longer able to ignore my thirst, I grab one of the bottles of water and start chugging. It is hard to drink in slow, moderate sips. My body is just too impatient and it tastes so good. I cannot possibly describe how satisfying and delicious water is when your body has been deprived of it for even as little as twenty-four hours. I swear, this is the first time in my life that I have actually tasted water, I mean, really tasted it - noticing the traces of metallic elements and the faint sodium aftertaste. I drink it with the acute sensitivity one typically reserves for wine or alcohol. I imagine a 100 plus proof Bourbon or a fine Cognac.

My mom always enjoyed a good Cognac and preferred Courvoisier VSOP. It was my token gift to her every Christmas for as far back as I can remember. She enjoyed it as an after dinner digestif, especially during the holidays but also on many other occasions that deserved special attention.

I remember one such evening a long while back when I was a teenager. I came home late in the evening after a night out, at a nearby lake, with my friends. My mom was in the den watching a late-night movie. I peered in to give her a nod of acknowledgement before going upstairs to my room. She waved her arms, motioning for me to come into the den, an excited look on her face.

"Come in", she said." I am watching Murder on the Orient Express and they are all in the dining car. Quick, go get two snifters of Cognac and we will have drinks with them". This was typical of my mom and movies. Always wanting to take part in them somehow, curious about what they were eating, wearing and comparing her likes and dislikes accordingly. She would love it out here. Whenever we went out to dinner she would choose a place where we could sit by the water. Okay, so this is a bit extreme. This is a far cry from a table by the water, but it is nice to think of it this way.

Night has arrived. It is quite beautiful out here, quiet, serene, a boundless deep blue of both sky and water. I imagine myself to be the only person on the planet, as though civilization never happened. No buildings, cars, trains, airplanes. Nothing, just an expanse of virgin space unscathed by the human presence except for me. Why am I here though? How did I get here and what would be the point of one specimen of one species existing? More than this, how did all of the existing species form in the first place? Why is there something instead of nothing?

The space around me is vast, endless but this is just one small ocean on an insignificant planet, floating within a tiny solar system, inside a single galaxy spiraling through an limitless sea of galaxies - billions of them! If I were a grain of sand, rather than an average sized human being, perched upon the hull of this boat, that grain of sand, together with all the grains of sand, in all of the beaches on this earth would not be enough to match the number of stars in the universe.

You might think - wait a minute - how do they know how many grains of sand there are in all of the beaches in all of the world. Well, they don't, they don't have to. All one needs to know is that the universe is infinite, but the earth and its sands are finite, that's all that matters, numbers do not even enter into it. It is the same with death. We know that our time on this planet is finite, for each and every one of us. It is the when and how that has an infinite number, or nearly so, of possibilities.

Here I am coming back to death again. I should really try to curb this habit. How did I start out talking about the remarkable taste of water and end talking about death and infinity? Kind of a no brainer really, look where I am. The middle of nowhere and nothing else to do but think. Although, thinking about death and infinity is far better than harboring the fear of death and infinity. Scrambling around frantically trying to create some sort of security only to succeed in meeting one's end more quickly. I do not know why, but I am not fearful. Sure, I know all of you psychologists are out there thinking. Well, my friend, fact is, you are fearful of death.

Your mind is simply burying this notion deep into your subconscious as a survival mechanism.

Really? What about all those times that I contemplated suicide? Hmmmm?

So, you have thought about suicide? Wow, join the club. You haven't ever attempted it though, have you?

Thought not.

Therefore, we can be quite certain that you have a fear of death like everyone else but it is stowed away, a stowaway fear perhaps.

Alright smart guy, I probably do fear death but it is a different fear now.

I could care less about the when. What worries me is the how. Suffering is the first concern. I do not want to suffer some long, drawn out death by disease (who does?). Even more dreadful is the possibility of some embarrassing stupid death. Falling off a ladder, for instance, or accidentally cutting my head off with a chain saw. I am anxious about winding up on the Darwin Awards website. If I were to chance across a genie in a bottle who granted me three wishes, the first would have to do with when I want to die, the second, how I want to die. As for the third, I would wish to find a genie in a bottle, every ten years - things change after all.

* * * * * * * * * *

Fuck it! I drank the three bottles of water today, just too damn thirsty. I have a pretty good understanding now of what dying thirst is and what it is like to be completely alone, totally isolated, with little to drink or eat. Seriously though, it's not like I should have to suffer miserably while I wait to be rescued. I mean, how ridiculous would it look if, when I am rescued, they find an emaciated figure who hasn't eaten or drank much for days only to discover that there was ample amounts of food and water inside the boat that was being saved in anticipation of a long wait out here at sea.

What an idiot!

I'll get more water and stuff tomorrow in the afternoon when I am burning up from direct sun and need the relief of cool sea water. For now, I am going to get prepped for the overnight. My poncho is completely dry, great, so I just need to rig myself to the boat and I will be all set.

Yesterday I collected some ropes and clips over the course of several dives. I the wound the rope twice around the boat and knotted it up top leaving a tail with a clip attached. This clips to another rope tied around my waist, which, when fastened, keeps me secured to the hull and allows me to sleep without having to worry about sliding off the side and sinking down to the ocean floor to rest for eternity.

Another spectacular evening has arrived. Without the interference of artificial light, the night is velvet black and it looks as though all the stars that exist are within sight. It is impossible not to be awed by this magnificence. The experience rivals every natural and man-made wonder and I cannot help but time travel as I sit here gazing up into the expanse. The beginning of it all. The Big Bang or whatever beginning you believe, it doesn't matter. It is stunning to ponder how all of this began. Equally stunning to ponder all that is here. How is it that so much exists when at one time there was nothing at all? Why all this diversity and restless life? Even more extraordinary is the fact that exposure to this night and this world instigates an endless array of philosophical questions that one rarely entertains in civilized life.

We are not accustomed to such thoughts, not most of us anyway. It is through the good graces of the arts and sciences (philosophy included in this of course) that any of this gets attention and yet, not to think of this would be no kind of civilization at all. Yet, to spend any serious amount of time grappling with such issues is considered, by many, foolishness. Such impractical use of one's time could only lead to idleness and confusion. Practicality is the battle cry of our modern world. Work hard, be industrious and prosper in the world of free market capitalism. Buy and sell, sell and buy, for there is infinite growth on this finite planet. All that is so far away at this moment, sitting here amongst these stars, not feeling alone, feeling more alive and sensing all of the surrounding life and energy that has been here for billions of years creates a profound alignment of the mind.

* * * * * * * * * *

I've studied, I've traveled, I've read everything I could get my hands on and nothing seems to satisfy me.
Like everyone else, I want to succeed, I want to improve but not necessarily in the terms that the world calls success.
Somehow, I've lost confidence in the accepted values

But I know that if I do find what I am looking for it will be something that I can share with others.

All your restlessness is of no concern my son, the world is restless.

As long as men set their ideals on the wrong objects, there will be no real happiness.

Not until men learn that it comes from within themselves. I know - that's not easy

The road to salvation is difficult to pass through, as difficult as the sharp edge of a razor

Passed another night out here on this floating hull with another movie clip. Day four, and I have to say, I am amazed that no one has come to rescue me yet. The old Chinese proverb comes to mind; "Careful what you wish for, you may just get it." It has only been four days though so what am I getting concerned about. I still have food and water trapped inside the cabin and, so far, I am in good spirits and good health.

It is odd though, I haven't seen so much as a bird out here let alone a plane high up in the sky or a cargo ship way off in the distance. I must be quite far from land, some part of the ocean where no one wants to be.

Where is that? Am I floating towards the South Pole? As I still do not remember anything about where I began this trip it is hard to say. Even if I knew where I had started out it would not help me all that much. There is nothing to work with here to get my bearings and this is a bit disconcerting to say the least. I like the idea that I am floating towards the South Pole and I am probably upside down right now.

Funny thing Gravity. One of the weakest forces in nature yet, no matter how hard I may try, I am unable to jump up into the clouds (or fall into the clouds). All this water, with a density and weight that measures into the millions or billions of tons, firmly secured to the planet, maintaining a perfect curvature. This certainly hints at just how massive this Earth is and what a small speck I must be relative to it.

On the contrary, I have spent most of my life concerned with my world in a wholly different scale than that of the Earth. One sees oneself so much bigger and the world so much smaller compared to the big life one is leading. We all do it, some of us quite a bit more than others, this administering of importance and degree of focus. Problems are big no matter what and we worry about how we will ever manage to resolve them, always prepared to take whatever steps are necessary as though our life depended on it, which it very seldom does.

Out here, it is solely the problem of staying alive and if that doesn't work out, so what - I die - problem solved. There is a kind of beauty in this. It is not like I want to stay alive because I have so much more I need to do before I am gone. Oh, there are things I want to do, sure, but does it truly matter after all? Will it change the world? Will it change me or those around me? If not, what the hell am I doing here anyway? I never thought about it so much. When I was young I never thought about whether there was a meaning to life or not. It just seemed obvious. I am here and there is stuff I want to do. I want to experience everything that I can. Taste all tastes, hear all of the sounds, see all of the sights and feel all there is to feel (or mostly all). I wanted to feed on life more so than direct it, there was plenty of time for direction. I can be anything I want. Besides, haven't I been told this all along?

"You can have it all"- "Just do it" - Be all you can be". Damn straight, that's right, that's me, this is my time, I deserve it.

* * * * * * * * * *

Made some dives this afternoon and I have four bottles of water and some crackers in a vacuum-sealed pouch. You think I would have retrieved the crackers two days ago when I had salvaged the cheese. Things are getting uncivilized out here. Perhaps a tuna will swim by so I can grab it and slice it up for my crackers. Haven't really seen any fish out here so far though.

What the heck?

All this ocean. Where the fuck are the fish?? Aren't they the least bit curious? It is not every day that some strange object is floating around for days on end. What the hell do these fish do all day anyway? I can't imagine that they are so busy that they have no time to swim up near the surface and see what this oblong, lifeless shape is overhead - stupid fish - fuck'em.

Obviously, I haven't taken my Damitol for a while and it is beginning to show. Even without the Damitol, I think I would be getting pretty hysterical right about now. It has been over a week and I am a bit on edge as nobody has been by and I haven't had anything but water for two days. No fish, no boats, no planes, no nothing!

Hey, Assholes!!! Finish your fucking coffee and get the hell out here already.

Can you believe this shit?

It has got to be ten days at least and still no one has come close to rescuing me.

So much for our "Information Age" - shit - the only information they care about is letting you know when the next sale event is. Lincoln's birthday? Hell, 40 t0 50 percent off storewide! Black Friday! Everything 50 percent and more!!

Just lost your job? We knew about before you did, come on down and get a special discount for unemployed shoppers!! There is so much information out there you need a cartload of apps just to organize it all never mind understand or utilize it in any significant way. I must have a hundred or more apps to help me be more productive and more organized and I hardly use any of them. They just sit on my home screen filling up space, creating colorful frames that make me look professional and cutting edge when all I really need is a "Beep Beep, wake the fuck up and find my boat app".

Yah, OK, I know I said that I did not want to be rescued too soon so that I could have a legitimate and life changing experience, but that was twelve days ago (I think) and this whole life changing thing is getting old. It is rough out here with no land in sight, no food to eat and water dwindling down to the last few bottles. Who knew that this would go on for so long? I certainly didn't and I certainly didn't plan on having to ration the water and food supplies I had on board. Three bottles of water and a can of beans that I have no way of opening so, in effect, I really have just three bottles of water. Not the worst scenario as one can live for about thirty days or so without food but only three or four days without water (why do I keep telling myself this). So, if I limit myself to two ounces of water per day, divided by three bottles of water, at sixteen ounces each, I can survive another 24 days out here and still be relatively worthy of being rescued. This seems perfectly doable and fits within a reasonable expectation for my being discovered.

Four more days added on to my ordeal and nothing further need be said other than that the days seem to be stacking up quite quickly. The first couple of days felt like an eternity, the gravity of the situation causing each hour to account for a full day and each day a month. Now, time has recalibrated and suddenly two weeks has elapsed and I have no recollection of such time passing. It must be that I am in and out of consciousness to such a degree that several hours pass and I cannot record them. I think about what happens with people who are slowly going crazy. The anxiety that accompanies the feeling that you are losing your mind builds to an unbearable pitch and then snap, your gone! The thought of losing your mind is no longer present. You are no longer capable of feeling like you are losing it. All that is over, you are in another state of mind that only others notice as off or irrational. In your mind, all is back to normal and there is a lasting peace again. Days drift past and there is nothing left that registers as anxious or crazy. I feel that now, a calmness and peace that allows for the days to pass without anticipation and fear. Perhaps this is the onset of death - it arrives without one being cognizant of it. No fear, no struggle, no real notice of your body letting go. It just lays you down gently and bathes you in light and lightness.

* * * * * * * * * *

I am staring at the can of black beans wondering how I can get it opened. I no longer have the strength to dive under the boat and swim into the cabin to salvage food and supplies- those days are over. I reach over to clutch the can, just hold it in my hand and imagine the taste and feel of the contents, but I clumsily fumble it and it falls into the water. Gone you might think, eh? But no. I have a line wrapped around it so that it would not be lost overboard while I slept. I smirk to myself as I reach down into the water to retrieve the can. Before I can grab it, I see the can rise up within a burst of bubbles and white foam, my whole body is propelled upward and pain seethes up through my right arm which, when I finally catch sight of it, has blood cascading down it and unspeakable pain wracks my entire being. I scream out from both pain and fright as the boat is nudged and jostled. I try to stabilize myself with my legs while holding my arm, blood everywhere and pouring into the water creating more frenzied behavior in the shark just below. I quickly glance down to see what is causing my pain and am relieved to see that the lower part of my arm and hand is still intact, but two fingers have been torn away by the ragged bite and shake of the shark. I pull at my shirt and tear it with my teeth in order to get it off my back and around my arm. This gets the bleeding under control and allows me to focus on securing myself to the boat and staying clear of the shark until he decides to look elsewhere for his meal. Soon he is gone and the quiet and calm of the ocean surface returns as though no threat had ever existed.

I am surely fucked now. This is turning into a horror movie instead of an uplifting survival tale. Time for a rewrite!! I yell to the emptiness.

Stop fucking with me!!

This, of course, helps tremendously.

Some people just do not realize how gratifying and cathartic screaming obscenities can truly be, especially in a situation like this. I mean, screaming Ouch! Please, why is this happening!! just doesn't cut it. Fuck has that ideally suited "f" sound to start off with. It allows the teeth to clamp down hard on the lower lip, fill with air pressure, perhaps even bubble and spit a bit, before bursting open into a wide mouthed roar - the vocal chords vibrating at full pitch, creating that guttural, rasping blast of sound that ends with the equally ideally suited "k" that forces that tongue up and towards the back of the throat where the final bit of air left in the lungs is released, short and sharp.

Shit! Can also be quite effective but this word is better for disbelief and is not, I find, fully effective when dealing with extreme pain or anger. Shit is great because you can hold onto the "sh" sound for any length of time, stretch it out for as long as you like and then finish it with a quiet "t" or a hard "t". The quiet "t" is more appropriate for disbelief while the hard "t" lends itself more to the "fed up" realm of emotion.

Then there is the commonly used "Fucking Shit! Which is highly prized for its three-syllable rhythmic quality, the "ing" useful as a buffer between the emphatic, visceral Fuck! and the air sweeping "sh" sound followed by the finality of "it". To miss out on these humble yet fulfilling delicacies is to be deprived of an expressiveness that is effective and wholly satisfying.

(Dear devoted reader, I am sure that you are appalled by my soliloquy at such an inopportune point in the story. But this really isn't the story yet. All of this simply represents thoughts and preambles leading up to the real story, so sit tight and allow me this transgression.

Sincerely,

Stranded, totally fucked human being)

I have secured myself to the ropes again and feel much better, although my hand is throbbing with pain still and the shirt that I have wrapped around it is soaked with blood. My snaggle-toothed friend has not been seen since so I decide to remove the shirt and rinse it out in the water, I wring it as dry as I can with one hand and wrap it around my wounded hand again. Staring down into the water I see that the can is still attached to the rope and discover that it has been punctured by the shark and a tooth remains stuck there in the can. It is the tooth of a "Carcharodon Carcharius"- a Great White. This conjures up the scene from Jaws where Hooper is explaining to the mayor what he found wedged in Bill Gardener's boat. I wish I could give the tooth to Hooper so he could show it to the mayor and prove just how big and dangerous this motherfucker is. Life is so like a movie, until it isn't.

Gripping the tooth and prying it back and forth allows me to forge a bigger hole in the can and I can spill it out into my mouth. This is so gratifying that the pain in my hand is temporarily dismissed. This is the first solid material that I have enjoyed in days and it tastes like nothing I have experienced before. Oh sure,

I have had black beans before, but these are not black beans now. These are tender bits of soft meat marinated in a silky-smooth gravy of lightly seasoned pureed truffles. I could eat the entire can but force myself to stop. Two weeks ago, I would have eaten all of it in one sitting and thought nothing of it, assuming, as I did, that rescue was soon to come and food was of little concern. I was still acting with the foresight of a politician back then but now I have been forced to proceed with vision and planning.

Too little too late of course, but at least I got the water part right, or as right as I could at this point. Nothing prepares you for this kind of thing. Growing up pampered and secure in the basic necessities of life, survival is not part of the thought process. Sure, there are still survival instincts that one develops over time. Instincts that prepare you for competition, such as, excelling at sports or getting good grades, finding a job and working towards a promotion. Basics of cooperation and social/professional networking. None of this has anything to do with life though, not the life we were meant to live.

Why does progress lead us away from nature, into an enclosed space, a sanctioned existence more isolated and singular with each technological advance? Why do we hear so much about progress and so little about where we want all of this to lead? The mainline Techno-Fantasy seems to be all about finding another habitable planet. How does this help with anything? If we do not adapt and evolve an intelligence capable of living in balance with this planet, what is the point of finding another? Are we to accept planets as floating Funhouses awaiting our arrival, their existence merely to appease our insatiable appetite for plunder. Is competition and gain our only drive? There cannot be meaning in this.

This can't be what we are here for.

Governments are no longer able to control the population by keeping people locked up in factories for 10 - 12 hours a day, that is solely for third world countries now and this is hardly tenable for much longer (fortunately). With no profit to be made in this country by the manufacture of goods, they are now in the business of manufacturing consent. Our consent to follow the order of the day, consume all that is put in front of us. Food and shelter is a given. We are encouraged to expand our wants and categorize nearly everything as needs. Ambition is equated with the drive for higher income, bigger houses, flashy cars and celebrated waste. What was once considered "making progress" has evolved to a point where, as volume rapidly increases and resources more quickly depleted, we find ourselves considering whether or not we can "survive progress". The ultimate irony of course. I am exhausted. I need a rest.

* * * * * * * * * *

- *Wait a minute. Is this all you do, just take it like this? What about your unions?*

- *No other union in the country'd stand for a thing like that. The waterfront is tougher, Father, like it ain't part of*
     America.

- *Do you know how a trigger local works?*

- *No. How?*

- *You get up in the meeting, you make a motion, the lights go out, then you go out. That's how it's been since Johnny and his cowboys took over the local. Name one place where it's safe to talk without getting clobbered.*

- *You know what you're letting yourself in for?*

It is morning and another dream/movie made its way into my head. They are growing more pertinent each time. The subconscious is magnificent in and of itself. I believe it must be an ancient survival mechanism. It speaks to us in our dreams and reveals truth, clear of the clouds of forgetting. It strips away our illusions and delivers the real in a manner that allows for true vision, a vision that cannot be fooled by the propaganda and insecurity society exerts on us. Don't get me wrong, in light of all that I have said, I am still an optimist relative to the future of our species. Why? Because I am a fool, and in the future, only fools will survive. I will expand on this later. The present is what is important here, more importantly, my present condition.

Roughly twenty-four hours have passed since my discovery of how to open cans in the middle of the ocean. All bleeding has stopped and the wounds are beginning to form scabs as the healing process takes over. I rip a clean piece of my shirt to make a new bandage for the area which once sprouted fingers. It isn't so painful anymore unless I touch, or worse, look at it. What will life be like now without two fully indexed hands? It is fortunate, if one can speak of fortune here, that it was fingers four and five. I grip the rope with my good hand and use only my thumb, index, and middle finger, in order to feel what it is like to have just these three to work with. Not so bad. I am able to hold the rope with plenty of strength and I think that I will be capable of doing most tasks without too much trouble. It is kind of like having the hand of a sloth controlled by the brain of a human, which is not all that different from my condition prior to the accident.

I decide to eat more of the black beans and fantasize about finer cuisine. They have dried up a bit since yesterday so I added a little water to the can and shake it gently. It oozes out of the can and slides into my mouth, again the sense of something solid creates an ecstasy throughout my body. This, I conjecture, could be a great enterprise to consider if/when I am rescued. Picture a Club Med type of atmosphere where people come, not for vacation but for deprivation, the severity of which is aligned with how much you are willing to pay. Clients are tethered off the coast on simple rafts made out of old wood pallets for anywhere from three days to three weeks. There they ponder the universe, or whatever, with only bread and water to survive. At the appointed time, they are reeled in and given their first full meal, nothing special, just some fresh fruit and vegetables, or perhaps, a hamburger (premium package). They eat and have an orgiastic experience like no other. They eat to their hearts content and then, depending on the package deal they signed up for, they are sent home or cast back out to sea for days or weeks. I am convinced that this would be quite a lucrative business with most clients coming back year after year. One could easily project that a certain percentage of clients would become hardcore addicts and remain indefinitely. The profit margin soaring to unexpected heights. One hundred years later, most moneyed people are living like this full time until their money runs out and they have learned to live this life completely on their own, a twelve-step program of sorts. "Welcome to Club Fed" where food is a luxury and life is a guessing game!

Maintaining a sense of humor is an important survival skill no doubt. I seem to want to goof around more and more with each miserable day that passes. So much of life is spent being serious, I sometimes think that this is what causes us to age. I know that science, in particular, genetic biology, has made great advances in the study of life and aging and what may cause the body to age - effects of oxidants, a particular gene, poor protein folding, or any of the truly enjoyable things in life. I maintain that seriousness is the ultimate killer. Whenever I meet someone who displays an absolute lack of humor I know they are not long for this world. It is a sixth sense and it instills health and longevity in those who indulge and practice humor.

(please refer several pages back to "being a fool")

Two more days have passed and things have taken a turn for the worse if, in fact this is possible. While changing the bandage around my hand I notice discoloring and the peculiar smell of rotting flesh. It seems that gangrene has visited me overnight and has decided feed of my hand. I have now entered the phase of survival where a person cuts off a leg, arm, or whatever in order to save their life. Without antibiotics, this is the only course of action left to me if this progresses any further. What is more disturbing is the fact that I have nothing to use to cut my hand off but the tooth of my friend Whitey Bolger. Of course, cutting off my hand only leads to an even bigger wound that would soon fester and become life threatening yet again. I suppose I could then sever my arm at the elbow and then wait for that to become acrid and proceed further up my arm. Not an entirely futile proposition though as each operation buys me more time until, unless rescued, it gets to the point where I must sever my head from my torso and then all is lost. Plus, there is the impossible odds of my being able to fully sever my head with a shark tooth before succumbing to bleeding to death.

Obviously, this is not an option to seriously consider. I do like the idea of attempting to cut off one's head in order to save oneself though. There is something philosophical in there somewhere.

OK, time to get serious. I remember being given a lovely rope of garlic before leaving. My friends know how much I enjoy cooking, especially when I am alone and have time to kill - oops, shouldn't have said that. One of my friends really hates when I use that phrase, preferring instead "downtime". I do not like downtime because it too closely references "being down" aka depressed and I am not interested in having depressed time. "Killing time" is a kind of Nom de Gare that insinuates conviction, the overthrow of time for your own device, a proactive (overused I know) attitude towards time that would otherwise be wasted. "Killing time" is especially good because for our entire life it is time that is killing us, therefore, what better way to exact revenge on time than by killing it.

"I, gallant Knight of the round(ish) table, hereby smote you villainous time and banish you to the realms of ennui, a threat no more to the sad and pitiful beings who wake, commute, work and die." And further more.......bonk!

Input any of a number of Monty Python sketches here and proceed. Alright, this time I will remain serious as things are really getting dire and I need to take appropriate action.

Garlic, yes, the garlic. As some of you may know, garlic is a natural antibiotic and what does one need when one's hand is ballooning, discolored and rancid? (besides a puke bag). Why antibiotics of course!

Oh, noble antibiotic

What

strength hath

thee   Unseen

yet known

To all who use you

Shit, why can't I stay serious here. I need to think this all through and do something. I'm fucking dying after all! I know I mentioned earlier that my diving days were over but I think I need to reconsider. At this point, if my diving days are over then my days in general are over and this is not how I want to exit this life. I envisioned something much more grandiose like saving someone off the subway tracks, rescuing a child from drowning, drinking three bottles of bourbon in one night, but not dying out in the middle of the ocean because of some errant storm that capsized my boat. I do not want to die like some bumbling fool. (I know I have admitted to being a fool earlier but that was a different fool - more on this later still). I will decide how and when I want to die thank you and I will kindly request that you, Mother Nature, mind your own damn business.

Garlic, garlic, garlic - stay with the program here. I must find it in myself to make one more dive and get the garlic rope. I know exactly where it is, I saw it twice on my previous dives. I just have to suck it up (no pun intended) and make another dive. While down there I can get one last stash of whatever food is still there. I wonder if Sharky is down there somewhere, lurking around waiting to see if I am smart enough to figure out that I need the garlic trapped under the boat for my wound and then make his move when he sees me dive in and under the boat. Those fuckers haven't lived for millions of years for nothing. I am going to have to take a chance. What does it matter anyway? All chances at this point are simply choices - no better or worse than any other as the option of doing nothing at all is most certainly death. I'll have the last of the black beans, practice my breathing, meditate (well maybe not that) and get myself pumped for this final dive.

Fucking right!!

* * * * * * * * * *

Back on board my capsized, totally fucked boat, and stoked to have a garlic rope and some Poptarts. I eat several cloves of raw garlic and take two more, crush them with the heel of my foot, and rub the mangled mess over my injury. Fuck yah, it hurts and it is a disgusting sight as well, the visual combined with the physical sensation makes for an excruciating experience but better this than no arm. Amen.

I repeat this treatment every hour or so (I don't know what constitutes an hour at this point, but I am giving temporal cues for your sake not mine). I could finagle a simple sun dial I suppose but what does time, or at least any measuring of time, matter now. I just need to know that dusk is soon to fall and get myself secured for the night. In the morning, tend to my wound and think about my predicament or ignore it for that matter.

No, there is no chance of ignoring it, but I can deal with it certainly, take it as a challenge. Will invisible, infinitesimal bacteria get the best of me or will I fight them with yet another biology groomed for this purpose. It's the little things that matter in life, in more ways than one. I am feeling pretty good about myself and confident that I will win this battle.

This wound is a positive though. Without this aliment to fight I would only have the fight for survival which is pretty much a waiting game, or would have been had it not been for Mack the Knife suffering from Overactive Jaw Syndrome. As a result of this injury, I have a definitive focus and purpose. One could even consider it a miracle, I mean, how many things could have happened that would have put an end to me or left me floating in the balance, careless and listless. I think now that someone is trying to save me seeing as the card playing Coast Guard isn't anywhere to be found. Perhaps my brothers, long deceased, have decided that now is the time, if ever there was one, to exert some heavenly pull and get my sorry ass off this ocean.

Whatever the case, I am determined to see this through and stay alive at least until the next challenge - or the next miracle. Maybe a whale will swallow me whole and harbor me in its womb until I have healed, then release me gently onto a placid beach to be discovered by gem- eyed island women eagerly attending to my body and nourishment. That would be a fucking miracle alright. Anyone listening up there?

I awake to bright sun and a burning sensation on the left side of my face. My simple poncho fabrication has blown off during the night, hanging useless off on the starboard side tangled in rope and flapping with an unnatural regulation.

Whatever skin that I had left on that side of my face has now, most certainly, been eviscerated - transformed into a leathery mass of coarse and cracking derma-plast. This is only a minor inconvenience though. My hand is burning as well, only not from the sun's generous ultra-violets, but from the infection that seems to be getting worse. I decide to mash up a whole handful of garlic cloves and pack the fleshy mass on top of the wound and wrap it up in a new cleaner piece of my shirt. If nothing else, this will make for a nice roast.

I can, with a certain amount of accuracy, say that I am completing my first month at sea. If you were to tell me, when all of this began, that I would be stranded for at least one month after my boat capsized I would have scoffed and shot a look of disgust followed by a hearty laugh and a gentle "fuck you". I still cannot believe it myself. One month adrift at sea on top of the bottom of my boat with two fingers missing, a bottle of water and one half Poptart. What a sorry state for someone so well equipped for emergency and so capable overall for anything that might come my way. What nonsense to be out here all this time. What area of miserable ocean have I foundered into? What unfortunate intersection of longitude and latitude have I pin pointed. These and other questions I hope to answer at some future date and then say to myself, "what are the odds and why did I win this particular lottery?"

Thinking about what I might say and do after I have been rescued is quite comforting and I allow myself to wander like some Flanuer of the psyche. How aggressively will I be courted by the media once I have returned. How will I cope with all of the attention after being so starved of social interaction. Perhaps there is no coming back from this, not fully anyway. I may have to live in seclusion for the rest of my life (if there is a rest of my life) and take on the menacing obsessions that plagued Howard Hughes. On a more positive note, I could live as a Zen monk delving deeper into the mysteries of consciousness and being. (Whoa!)

Of course, there is the other extreme that seems more likely. I return home after this exhausting ordeal and I am courted by every news outlet that exists. I play to the crowd and play up my story to the extent that I believe myself to be something more than I am and everybody loves it - I love it. I exhaust myself now in a manner close to, if not entirely the same as, what I had suffered at sea. Morning shows, radio shows, podcasts, Twitter feeds, etc, etc. The bottle of bourbon empties more quickly and amphetamines start taking their toll. I collapse finally and wake up in the hospital with an array of tubes and sensors attached. I am miserable and weak. I long to be back on the ocean fighting for my life, a life worth fighting for. As the music fades in and reaches a crescendo I flail and roar while detaching myself from the spidery legs of the monitoring devices crowded all around me. The music fades out and my head pitches back, rolls from one side to the other and my eyes fix on the ceiling, wide open and glossed over with impending death. All is white and then absolute black.

Yah, that's the way it will be no doubt - I'm no fucking hero.

* * * * * * * * * *

Chaulk up another night at sea and another morning of bright sun burning the last layer of skin off my nose. Even if I survive this ridiculous ordeal I will undoubtedly die of skin cancer before long. I am really feeling weak and so depleted of energy that I cannot even bother to hope.

Hope is for the lazy and demoralized and I am not lazy or demoralized per se, just weak. All I can do is lie here and gaze. I cannot think anymore. I cannot dream either. My sleep is empty now. I am not even sure that I sleep. My conscious mind is indecipherable from my unconscious mind. Although, one cannot define sleep as a lack of consciousness, can one?

Shit – see - I am trying to think and it is a waste of time. I am better off staring up at the sky with the objectivity of a camera. I have never experienced such release as this, a letting go that is far beyond any kind of selective choice. I am no longer capable of choosing any action over another or any thought over another. I can only open my eyes or close my eyes and I do not consider this something I choose to do anymore. So, I lie here with my eyes open and lie here with my eyes closed - open - closed - open - closed.

An array of meaty clouds have formed overhead. Mashed potatoes, as a young child once put it to me. Aah, meat and mashed potatoes. Gravy and bisquits. Cheese and wine. Prosciutto and melon. Cake and scream. Bullion and cigars. Coftea and cockroaches. Mold and fruit flies. Pingles and dribbles and hippies and sippies......som..th....wha....uuh.

Clouds.... big.... puffy.... White... cotton.... cloudssss... Heaven?.... Hello, is that you?

So, slow these massive, morphing mammoths. Farewell. Fare thee well. Fuck off.

I am dying and happy to be giving in to it fully. I love death. I embrace death. Death is peace, joy, comfort, a beautiful sleep.

AAAAAAHHHHH.....Shit.... What now! C.C. is back to eat me before I have had a chance to pass away peaceably.

No....no, no, something else. Something else altogether. Whatever it is it is much smaller, hardly a threat even. It came out of the sea for sure - it must have.

Forced from my death revelry I use every bit of strength I have to sit up and look about me. There in my lap lies a floundering fucking fish!! Yes, a fish. A flying fish (I will dispense with the Latin term for it) - a live fish has fallen into my lap.

I cannot possibly have a fish in my lap!

I am most certainly dead and this is the loving attempt by death to lead me out gently. I knew death was generous and sweet. I knew it wouldn't be some hellish rancor cast upon us as some kind of punishment. The beauty of life is that it offers up death in the end. Death is a reward a *fait accompli*. This beautiful fish is in my lap offering itself to me for nourishment. It is a God come down from those beautiful clouds. I grab it quick and hold it in my hand (the good hand of course). I bite its head off and revel in the ecstasy of flesh and wetness. It doesn't need salt! It doesn't need "fresh basil with a light butter sauce". It doesn't need anything but my overwhelming desire to tear at it, chew it (barely) and gulp it down. Holy shh......this is a miracle. The miracle of the fishes. I am fucking Jesus and I have summoned this fish from the ocean and shall eat of its flesh. After devouring this ichthy-miracle I have a look around. Feeling somewhat revived, I cannot help but think again. This is good, as thinking usually leads to something useful and I feel the need to be useful again.

Scanning the area of my immediate surroundings I find that several more fish are here with me, caught up in all the jeremiad rigging I have been using to keep myself secured to the hull. It is imperative that I hold on to these beauties. I take off my pants, which are shorts at this point, and knot the pant legs. I rear the pants up close to one of the fish and scoop it into the pant leg. I do this with the remaining three fish, spool a rope through the belt loops and cinch the waist shut. I lower the pants into the water. My life support system securely in place, I lay back and rest.

* * * * * * * * * *

Awake and confused. The light is faint. I am not sure if it is the early evening of the Day of the Fishes or the following morning. I suppose it could be early evening the following day as well. Hell, it could be two days later for all I know. I feel rested and a little stronger. It must be the next day. I check the life support and my miracles are still there, alive and healthy. Within seconds I have the head of one in my mouth. Joy, utter joy and contentment.

In a single day, I have become quite the connoisseur of fresh fish. This goes well beyond Sushi in that the eating of this delightful fish happens while it is still alive. The sight of it is so tantalizing that there is no time or desire to think. One just eats, without grace or ceremony. The eyeballs are delectable. Yes, shiny rubbery fish eyes are like little balls of candy.

I do not exaggerate. I recall many years ago, a friend of mine, a Frenchman, was attending a rooftop soiree. A platter with a very large brazed fish was laid out on the table. Everyone was delighted with the spectacle of this huge, delicious looking fish, commingled with vegetables and fresh herbs. My friend let out an avid "aaahh" then reached down, plucked out the eyeballs and gulped them down with a most satisfying grunt. Horrified, all those in close proximity (including me) scrunched their eyebrows and stretched their lips wide. No one could speak. The Frenchman gave a hint of a shrug and walked off.

Today, this very moment, I would challenge my friend to a duel of fish eye eating and enjoy it immensely.

The World and All That It Implies

Chapter 5   **The Storm**

Great masses of clouds today - Cumulus clouds. The Buddhists believed them to be the spiritual cousin of the Elephant and one can certainly see why. I have gained great appreciation for these Gaseous Gargantuans. This is not the first time that I have given clouds my fond attention. Many years ago, while visiting friends in New Mexico, in an attempt to get out of a creative slump and perhaps find some inspiration for a water tower, I had been awed by the clouds that formed throughout the day. I kept track of their movement as they sailed across the sky, sometimes very low and spread wide, other times, soaring high up, arranged in finger-like columns. Sunsets transformed them into spectacles of rich color, sensational but fleeting, lasting a mere twenty minutes at most.

Hovering over me now, these cauliflower hubs unfurl and expand with a solemnity that is captivating. Seated beneath them I indulge in some quiet cloud busting. I concentrate on the upper section of the cloud, fix my site and bust it open. The cloud will do this regardless of my intentions, but it is a relaxing and enjoyable exercise that makes me feel as though I am actually accomplishing something. I do this for a while (don't ask me how long as I no longer have a sense of time). I am relieved to be doing something simply for the pleasure of it although I am acutely aware of the fact that this is short lived.

Off on the horizon I see what look like Cumulonimbus. If I am correct about this, then I had better keep a tight watch on their development. Cumulonimbus clouds are the most threatening (yes, clouds can be threatening) species of clouds that the earth and atmosphere produce. Cumulonimbus, the King of Clouds, at its full capacity can be larger than Mount Fuji. Considerably larger in fact, their summits reaching to 60,000 feet in some cases, with an energy equaling an atomic bomb or two. These clouds are carrying some serious arsenal as well, the hail that forms inside being large enough to put serious dents, if not holes, in aircraft (not to mention the head of an unfortunate chump stranded at sea). As I peer off into the distance, it seems that just this type of cloud variety is coming my way and the sky is looking grim. The light is veiled by a growing intensity of clouds and another kind of light is emerging. It is an ominous greenish light that seems to hover just above the surface of the ocean. It advances rapidly and envelopes everything like a thick fog.

Huge bursts and a cackle of crackling electricity fills the air. Time to prepare for a storm. Not that there is much I can do. I check all of the ropes and tighten any that need tightening. I eat the remaining fish in my pants and tie myself to the hull. I am not convinced that this is the best idea. The boat could sink and drag me down with it or it could stay afloat and save my life. Is it even a fifty-fifty chance? It could very well be a sixty forty or quite possibly a seventy -thirty, there is no way to tell. I no longer put my faith in math. The universe is random and fate is fixed.

The storm is closing in and whipping up great gusts of wind. The water below is a dark as coal with bright white tufts spilling over into black again. Great heaping swells are present now and I pitch back and forth and up and down. I cannot keep my head from slamming back against the boat and my legs and arms feel stretched to their limit - I should dislocate every joint before long. Blasts of water and foam assault my face and breathing dry air is nearly impossible. I engage with an endless routine of gulping air and water, choking and coughing - gulping, choking, coughing.

The swells have gained in height and each time I rise up I see nothing but darkness and clouds. The horizon is indistinguishable, and the sky lights up with such intensity that I am momentarily blinded. I do not feel fear so much as curiosity. I cannot imagine what will be the worst of it. Is this as bad as it will get or am I in for a display of awesome power and energy that will swallow me up before I have time to witness it - a sudden pounding and blast of light that eviscerates everything in an instant and leaves behind the faint murmur of human life being extinguished. Another swipe of wind and the boat leaves the water completely, cast upward, swirling around and flipping over. I am facing the water as the boat crashes back down upon the surface and instantly the world shuts off.

The World and All That It Implies

Chapter 6   **The Beaching**

I was barely awake when I heard a faint kind of licking, lapping sound. Deja vu?

Yes, most assuredly.

Only this time I know it isn't Finley. This time I have sand in my mouth and eyes and everything is stationary - relatively speaking. I roll over slowly and I don't even bother to open my eyes. I know where I am. I am on terra firma and that is all I know and care to know. I am comforted by the fact that nothing is moving beneath me. There is plenty moving over and above me but nothing beneath. I love this sensation and I am happy to lie here and enjoy it. The air is dry and there is a light breeze caressing my skin. I can hear birds above the fussy water and their notes ring like love. I could lie here forever and bask in this stillness.

Inertness is the most wonderful, desirable state.

Ooooohhhh......fuck me. My head is heavier than my boat. My whole- body aches like a son of a bitch and my legs are like heavy rubber boots. Am I really going through all of this shit again? Waking from a clueless stupor, fumbling around for balance and questioning my surroundings, speculating as to whether or not I am dead.

This is getting old, I manage to get to my knees and have a look around. Nice trees (I already pointed out the birds) and some boisterous growth below them. I stare across and down the coast line for a long time - just staring -perfectly still. Trees sway and the surf slides over the sands but nothing else is in motion. I do not see any sign of an animal at ground level. Some crabs here and there but no four-legged, furry (or otherwise) animals. I feel like Dorothy after falling into Munschkinland, flora but no fauna, but hiding all around are creepy creatures waiting to reveal themselves when the moment feels right. I decide not to wait for them and proceed to lift myself to my feet. This takes some considerable effort as well as a remarkable ability to ignore pain. I lift my leg, throw myself off balance and plant my foot back down. I have taken the first step (tempting here to reference the Apollo landing although their steps were much lighter). Not so bad. I give it another try and succeed in taking another step. It is slow and arduous, but man does it feel good to be walking. The sand is easy on my feet and helps to anchor me each time so that I keep my balance rather easily.

I am walking without the least concern for where I am going, glad to be walking and moving in a direction away from the water. That fucking ocean can fuck off. I don't want to hear its lapping, licking shit anymore and I don't want its salty scum on my skin either - puuuuthh - I spit on you. I decide to head for the tree line and find a shady area to sit and reflect. Each step is a chore and can only be done by stopping between each step and taking a couple of deep breaths.

I should be able to make it there by the end of the day. Surprisingly, before long, I have made it to the shade and found a hospitable rock to sit my ass down. All this before sunset, brilliant.

I am quite proud of my achievement thus far and I take a moment to acknowledge it before doing any other activity. I have a look at my injured hand. The garlic seems to be doing the job, but the bandage is old and crusty and needs replacement. I am too tired to deal with this now.

If I am going to have any sort of success on this island I will have to address my needs, with regards to nutrition and strength, as soon as possible. I look around and do my best to focus and observe details in my immediate surroundings. There are Palm trees mostly, along with an array of smaller leafy trees that I do not recognize. At my feet, there exists a plethora of debris consisting of coconut husks, bark, leaves and an accumulation of smaller unidentifiable bits and chunks, all of which combine to create a course but spongy inland floor.

Every so often I hear rustling and cracking off in the distance but no evidence yet of any creatures other than birds and flies. There are all kinds of flies and insects crawling and buzzing around, curious about the strange solid, odd scented, warm blooded mass inhabiting their space. I, in turn, am curious (mildly) about what oddities are inhabiting my space. Are we to get along with one another in the days, weeks, years (please no) that lie ahead? More importantly, will any of these little lives contribute to sustaining my life, as food or otherwise. I look off to the left and see an odd colored form and then realize that it is more than an odd colored form, it is my boat!

Fuck'in eh. What do you know - my boat - we both survived. I now have the motivation to develop a course of action and, once again, it involves getting to the contents of my boat.

83

History does in fact repeat itself. As for the plan, screw it. I am in no state to get to the boat anytime soon. I take the attitude of "put off 'til tomorrow what you cannot possibly do today" and decide to work on getting myself setup with some kind of shelter and a bed, of sorts, to sleep on. Palm leaves are perfect for shelter. Unfortunately, they are also quite heavy and cumbersome even for a person in a normal state of health and well-being which I am decidedly not. The best activity for me at this point is one that allows me to be seated, so I proceed to gather a few of the palm leaves within reach and commence with stripping them of their fronds so that I am left with several strong, pliable sticks to use for support. This takes some time (hours probably but, as you know, I am incapable of measuring time with any accuracy) to complete this task but now that it is done I am ready to move on to the next task.

This requires my standing attention, so to speak, so I ease myself up to a vertical position, take a couple of steps towards a full palm leaf and using one of my palm sticks, I slide it between the fronds and drag it over to the spot where I plan to rest for the night. I repeat this activity until I have six large palm leaves. I pair up two leaves and start weaving the fronds together (as seen on TV). This creates a strong weave of the two leaves and after doing this with the remaining four leaves I now have an effective covering for the roof of my dwelling. Now all I need is my dwelling. I create a lean-to by positioning my palm sticks between the ground and the weave. This makes for a nice shelter that directs any rain that may fall from collecting and collapsing the roof with its weight. I collect more palm leaves. Some are stripped for use as supports and some are paired and woven together.

Soon I have a cozy enclosure with a large opening at the front that faces out towards the ocean. All around my enclosure I have balanced palm sticks in such a way that, should any animals (or humans?) come lurking around, the sticks will fall and crash against my hut, waking me up so that I may defend myself if need be. Clever eh? Pretty crude and useless most likely.

I manage to finish while there is still some light and, needless to say, I am exhausted and ready for sleep. This does not take much preparation at all. I am much too tired to worry and therefore, any trepidations I might have about going to sleep on a strange island with little or no protection is of no consequence.

The light has returned, and no sticks have fallen against my shelter. I peer outside and see that the ocean is still there, and I am alive and well (sort of). I hope that this is not a dream but even if it is, who cares, it is most enjoyable regardless. The sun is quite high. It must be noon or later, which means that I have been sleeping for some time - probably ten hours or more. Remarkable how different it is to sleep on firm ground rather than bobbing up and down constantly at the whim of the sea. My mind and body has improved immensely overnight, the melatonin having a good chunk of time to make its repairs. I cannot believe my luck. A month or more stranded at sea, a fortuitous storm casts me out of the ocean and onto this island where, as far as I can tell, life will continue - my life.

Today's schedule, as you may recall, revolves around my getting to the boat which, luckily, was also cast ashore. I am feeling quite fit this morning/afternoon (whatever) and see no reason why this task cannot be completed before nightfall.

The boat is no more than one hundred yards away and figuring that I can walk about one yard (one step) every ten seconds or so it should take but one hour to reach the boat (I know it is just under seventeen minutes but if you did not question my calculation then start paying attention). I know that I cannot make this trip without stopping several times to rest and gather my strength (Hah, so my original calculation is more accurate).

I try to observe everything in my path as well as the vicinity that I can reach with my eyes. Nothing new yet. The crabs are looking very tasty and as I walk I think about various methods for catching them. Water is on my mind (duh) and I am hopeful that some remained trapped in my boat. The closer I get the more I anticipate both joy and despair. What if there is nothing left? What if that damn shark is hiding out in there? What if that isn't even my boat, just some wishful illusion that I cannot get rid of. Perhaps the boat will always be one hundred yards away and I will be forever walking towards it until I finally pass out and die.

Shit.... there I go.... not even one full day on the island and already death has to start chattering. Not going there.

Yes, the boat exists. I am gaining on it. I will be there soon, and everything will be as it should be. I am confident that there will be provisions still contained inside. One more minute to rest and then I will push on for the last ten yards or so. My excitement builds, and I no longer want to use the full minute to rest. I move on and soon I am standing at the bow. The boat is still capsized (fucker), I give it a light kick and listen...... nothing

I do not know what I expected....ouch maybe...or "Hey, WTF, I'm sleeping in here."

I reach down and attempt to lift and right it but nothing doing. I am too weak. I stand still and stare off into the distance, hoping that out there somewhere is help, a suggestion, kind of like what Moses experienced when he came across the burning bush.

"I am that I am, and you are fucked"

I am fucked. If I cannot get inside this boat my hope of relief from thirst and starvation is pretty much nil.

Looking off towards the tree line I do in fact find an answer. I need to get over to those palms and find a fallen tree, small, light, but strong enough to act as a lever to pry the boat up and over. This can work, and I need to get over there pronto (obviously, pronto is unlikely) and drag back a palm trunk.

Mission accomplished but I need to rest before I can think about raising the boat. I sit and gaze out over the ocean.

Man, what a delight to be seeing it from land. It has only taken a day and I am able to see beauty in it again. The light sparkling off the surface and the beautiful, calm shush of the surf. It doesn't take long before I get antsy and decide that it is time to try my luck with the raising of the boat.

I grip the log firm and push it under the boat as far as I can. The sand jams it up and I pull it out and push it back in again. Several more of these actions and the log is half way under the boat. I take a breath, grab the end of the log and heave upwards. I get it raised about a foot and then collapse - nothing doing - I cannot get it any higher. I make another attempt with the same results - maybe a little higher than the first time but not significantly so. It is clear to me after two attempts that I am not going to be able to do this.

Plan B

I will gather together an assortment of rocks and use them as wedges between the sand and boat, gradually getting it high enough off the sand so that I can crawl under and get whatever might be left in there.

This is not going to happen today. I am pitifully slow and the light is already showing signs of moving on. My goal is to collect the rocks that I need and set them next to the boat ready for use in the morning. I create a ramshackle sled out of woven palm leaves which allows me to slide a few rocks at a time over to the boat. This chore lasts well past the light, but my eyes are adjusted well enough to see what I am doing. I just need one or two more trips and I will be set. Back at the shelter and feeling good about the day's events. I am sore but glad to know that I have some modicum of strength to carry out these duties. Tomorrow I will apply my hoisting technique and get myself under the boat and into the cabin. All that lay ahead for this evening is rest and cellular reparation.

* * * * * * * * * *

Two nights consisting of sleep upon a fixed, motionless bed.

This is helping my body and mind as much as food, motivation is returning with great speed. Time to head for the boat. Why didn't I sleep next to the   boat and save walking to and fro? Who knows, I can't think of everything. I am already settling in to creature comforts I guess. I like the idea of a home base - a place to recoup and separate from the rational, pragmatic self.

Made it to the boat and I am left with plenty of energy to begin my task. I put a couple of rocks next to the log and slowly pry the boat up off the sand. Resting the log on my shoulder as I kneel on the sand, I reach over and push a rock under to ledge of the boat then push the log off my shoulder.

So far so good.

I use a three, two, one approach with the rocks, laying down three rocks first, then stacking two on top of them, and one on top of the two - a pyramid scheme so to speak. I work this method to each side of the log and now I have a crawl space of about a foot and a half. This is enough to get under the boat and inside the cabin. I start my crawl, being careful not to bump the boat or disturb the rocks as this whole contrivance is quite precarious and one bump could dislodge the boat and entomb me for good.

I reach the cabin area and scoot inside. It is very dark, the light barely reaching this far. I remain still and give my eyes time to adjust. I imagine myself a cheerless cave dweller, alone in one of the smallest recesses of the cave, brush in hand, prepared for an existential act. How did they see in there - a torch would not be prudent as this would eat up what little oxygen existed in such a small space.

There was a story I read many years ago, about a German prisoner of war who had been put in solitary confinement with no light at all. He later wrote of this experience and remembered being completely blind initially. Each day his eyes adjusted to the dark and he began to regain some of his vision. After about a month, he was able to see his surroundings, the cement floor and where it met the wall, the corner where his food was always placed and the scattering rats that previously he could only hear.

I lay still and ponder such an experience. Surely, I cannot wait a month for my eyes to adjust but this is not necessary as there is ample ambient light to allow satisfactory vision after a few minute's time. While I wait, I try to remember where I stored the essentials. I have a waterproof bag with matches, a lighter, burners, first aid shit and a cigar or two. I think about the cigar, the nutty, smoky curl of tobacco on my tongue. Man, that is good.

I can see a cabinet and reach to open it, amazed to see that is closed after all of the shit the boat has been through - must make a note of the latch company.

I open it up and find that it is empty. The door must have opened then slammed shut again during the tumultuous tumbling, probably more than once – forget making a note of the latch company. Next cabinet - empty as well.

I consider the drawers. There are two that are close enough for me to see and I open them both - nothing. I am discouraged to say the least and I express this by throwing the drawer across the cabin. I hear a quiet creaking sound and immediately regret throwing the drawer as it sounds like the boat is about to dislodge and fall back down upon the sand thereby trapping me for good while forming a neat little sarcophagus for my remains.

I wait and listen - silence again. Great - I survived my foolish tantrum and begin looking around for anything of value. Towards the back, I can see a faint bluish color, it looks like there is something wedged in the corner where the bed is. I can see it because the mattress is white (dark grey in these conditions actually) so the blue, although greatly desaturated, is clearly distinct against it. I wiggle gingerly towards the back of the cabin and reach for the bag.

Fantastic, this is the waterproof bag. Yay, and fucking Yay again! This is my life line. I can make fire and cook.

I remove myself from the cabin and emerge from the boat with much optimism. My eyes succumb to the extreme brightness and I have to shut them and lower my head towards the sand. It takes several minutes before I am able to open them again but once I do, I am delighted to see the waterproof bag and all of its contents.

I run (this consists of taking four or five steps within a ten second period) back to my domicile and wallow in my good fortune. Knowing that I have fire and can cook food is so satisfying that my hunger is satisfied as well. I start mulling through all the recipes for crab and fish that I have stored in my memory and this fills me full of virtual nourishment.

I go back out and collect rocks for building a fire pit. This I complete with minimal effort and soon my pit is ready for action. I rummage for deciduous debris and throw most of it into the pit. Sprinkle with dry leaves and bark, light and done. FIRE!

Raging fire actually, and a warmth that comforts me to the bone - enveloping and womb-like.

Fire is, undoubtedly, the most powerful connection with our primal instincts. Harnessing this energy and having control over when and where to use it set our species off on a path to both progress and destruction. Fire has always had a magical component associated with it because of its power to create, destroy and regenerate. We are the only species to have brought this prodigious spirit under control and there is, clearly, a magic to it. A profound, enigmatic rapture that fire inspires. This burning, glowing offspring of the sun is what secures my survival on this island and I am imbued with energy and strength that I have never felt until now. It is time to gather some sea fare for cooking.

I grab one of the palm sticks and head out along the shoreline towards an area where some rocks protrude. There I find a community of crabs scurrying around blowing bubbles and playing hide and seek. It is a simple thing to catch them. I lower the end of the palm stick into a crevice in the rocks, the crab swiftly locks on to it and I lift it up and smash it against the rocks. Crude but wholly effective. I repeat this act until a half a dozen crabs are laid out next to the rocks. I wrap them in a palm leaf and head back to the hut.

The fire has calmed to a slow, even burn. I wrap two more palm leaves around the leaf containing the crabs and throw it onto the fire. A big puffing sound and a flit of sparks rise up and swirl above the pit. It looks like I have conjured a spirit. While my crusty crawlers simmer, I take a look at my injured hand and grab some fresh palm leaves to wrap around it. I know - palm leaves, palm leaves, palm leaves, but this is what is close at hand and this is what works.

The crab stuffed leaves are smoldering steadily and I reckon it is time to have a taste of my magnificent bounty. I put a couple of long sticks together and slide them under the leaves. With a quick upward jab, the contents of the pit lift out and flop to the ground. I throw some sand over it and then start stabbing and poking at the smoking bundle. I reach the last layer and unveil a lovely stock of red/black crabs still simmering in their shells. They are too hot to eat but I am content to just stare at them for now.

Meanwhile, thirst is making itself known and I consider my options for finding water before nightfall. I was hoping to find some in the boat, but I guess I got all that there was prior to washing up on the island. I can't remember what I had or did not have prior to this. The crabs have cooled. I crack open the body of one and shovel the contents into my mouth, instantly a warm, tingling sensation fills my mouth and body. Ecstasy again, like the black beans of the week before (or however long ago it was).
Sooo... fucking good.

I finish all of the crabs and could probably puke but I take my mind to another thought in order to divert this feeling, that being, the need for water.

While accomplishing my tasks over the last two days, I had a number of good looks at the island from the shoreline. Several hundred yards or so inland, there rises up a huge wall of vine and rock that peaks at about two thousand feet to best of my judgement. It does not form a point, it is a rim that stops abruptly and looks about six hundred feet wide. A strange formation indeed.

With a structure like this, water has to be cascading down somewhere and I need to get over there and find it. Feeling energized and sprightly (aka delusional), I pick up the waterproof bag and head for the wall. This will take some time and it is clear that I will not be returning here to sleep, I will have to build another shelter when I reach my destination. I figure that I will be building a series of domiciles all over the island as I venture further each day.

Standing at the base of the wall/mountain, looking straight up, I know instantly that I will not be climbing this sucker any time soon. Best I can do is start moving around it and see if there are any waterfalls or pools of fresh water to be found. It is not easy to walk along here as there is much overgrowth and I need a machete in order to make any kind of path through this stuff. I need to find water though, so I will have to make the best of it and fumble along the perimeter of the wall until I find "la source".

The sun is getting low and my arms and legs are scratched and bleeding. Insects of all kinds are feeding on me, especially the bloody areas and I have a achieved a degree of misery beyond all expectations. Swiping at flies while losing and regaining balance constantly is labor intensive, and I am growing weak and disgusted. I stop and for a while and rest. All I hear is heavy breathing and I feel it acutely. I drop my head and one small droplet of sweat winds its way down the bridge of my nose and descends to the ground. Normally I would have copious amounts of sweat pouring down my face, arms and back, but there is little excess fluid in my body for this. Lifting my head up I prepare to move on when I hear a faint trickling sound. At first, I fear that it is the sound of my brain melting and trickling out of my head but an instant later I realize that I am hearing water. It has to be water. I have heard no other sound like this since arriving on the island. I could be hallucinating but I think I am too tired to hallucinate (if that makes any sense). I move on and soon there is a slight clearing and a small area that looks like a pool of water. Yes, absolutely it is.

I flail and hop and move anxiously towards this vision anticipating unspeakable relief. As I reach the pool I stretch out my arms like an eagle and surrender myself to the water below. It splashes - it is wet, it cascades down my neck and back - it is water. Fucking water!
Clean, Pure, Cool, Life Giving Water.(I sound like a Poland Springs ad) Fuck off, you can't bottle this shit.

Lying back on the bank my body is experiencing pain and relief - both extremes and both extremely felt. Another miracle, another lucky fucking break. I never had this kind of luck in my life before. Never have I been so thankful. I observe the clouds and think back to my time on the boat, near the end, when I thought it was the end and all I could do was stare up at the clouds. Now look at me.

Beneath these clouds again and feeling like life is beginning anew. I am going to reinvent myself and my life here avoiding) all my life. My sailing adventure to find myself has brought me to this island. It is here that I am meant to live and prosper. Have I really anything to go back to?

The World and All That It Implies

Chapter 7   **Making A Living**

I have found a sweet spot half way between the shore and the
pool. I spent the last few days clearing and preparing the area for a
more permanent living space and have built a quasi- foundation of
rocks stacked a foot high and forming a circle that is roughly ten
feet in diameter. I plan to make posts by combining a dozen palm
sticks and binding them with rope made from the vines. I will put
these posts around the foundation at three- foot intervals and then
construct hemisphere trusses crisscrossing the expanse from one
side to the other to support a roof of palm leaves.

The dome shaped structure is one of the strongest and most economical for the building of a shelter. Good 'ol Buckminster Fuller would be proud of me (but horrified by the craftsmanship).

I am proud of me (sort of) and happy to be building a home. What is it Bachelard said? "One does not build a home in which to live, one lives to build a home" - or something similar.

I am indeed living to build my home. That is all that is on my agenda and it is all that motivates me.

Funny to think that I have been an architect for some twenty years and I am just now building my own home. It is fitting that this home should be so small and basic, built solely for living, not impressing, not for storing three cars and a bunch of shitty junk. I think this is one of my proudest achievements and no one will see it but me and that is as should be.

The shelter is complete and I am fully stocked with water, coconuts and crabs. Each day brings greater strength and greater enthusiasm for this life. I feel strong enough to return to the boat and lift that fucker up and over finally.

So that is what I do.

I accomplish this with an ease that would have been fantasy when I first landed here.

With the boat upright, I have ample light and can see

everything in the cabin. It still smells like low tide and there are life forms crawling everywhere. I look around and begin opening up all of the cabinets again. Just as before, they are all empty. I open the drawers and find a pencil, a pen, some computer cables, a map, sunglasses (cool) and some paper clips (why the hell are there always paper clips?) I put these items into the waterproof bag and resume my search. There, above the bed (or what's left of it) still attached to the wall is my machete - thank Christ.

Most of the rope that I had used to secure myself to the boat is still here, tangled all about but in good shape none the less. I whack at knots with the machete and detach all of the ropes, gather them in loops and throw them over my shoulder. A few scant glances to confirm that I have got all that there is here and then I head back to The Dome - my home (that is its name). My home the dome, yes, life has a certain poetry to it.

I am back at The Dome with fire (matches anyway), a machete, rope, food and water. I am kicking ass! In a few days' time, I may even be ready to scale the Big Green Monster.

The Green Monster, ah yes, I fall back into a reverie of Fenway Park, Kenmore Square and the Citgo sign. It is nothing but a romantic thought though, I don't really like baseball. It is America's sport alright. Long, eventless and costly. How can you call something a sport if the game is routinely spent chewing tobacco or gum. It is a great profession though. If I were going to strive to be a professional athlete, I would definitely be a professional baseball player. You don't have to run much, you don't have to sweat much and you won't beat the hell out of your body, rendering it useless later in life for anything other than daydreaming about the good 'ole days.

Yah, baseball would be the way to go.

"Take me out to the ball game....." no, no, get that right out of my head.

Having spent the morning making plans and supplying myself with a hearty breakfast, it is time to pack some things and prepare for a full day of island reconnaissance. From what I have observed thus far from the shoreline, the island thins to a kind of tail at the opposite end and there is not much growth. I decide to head in that direction, staying along the shore. It is a stretch no more than two miles, I'm guessing, and I reach the point where it trails off into the ocean in about four hundred and forty wave breaks, or forty- four minutes, this being roughly ten wave breaks a minute, which is now my preferred method for time as it is far simpler than counting seconds (remember, I could care less about time, this is for your benefit really).

Looking back towards the island I can see both sides and I get a good sight of its overall shape and topography. At the opposite end is the Big Green Monster and the shore line hugs closely all around it. This is the widest part of the island and looks to be about a mile wide with massive growth all around. I imagine what this might look like viewed from above. I move all of the spatial cues around in my head and come up with something that resembles a comma or paisley shape.

I have a few sips of water and stuff a chunk of coconut in my mouth (to suck on rather than chew) and head back along the other side of the island. I stay along the perimeter to keep things simple and alternate my gaze between the ocean and the tree line. The interior of the island needs far more time to investigate and will have to be scheduled for another walk. As I approach the far end I forge a route around the outskirts of the mountain. The shore reduces considerably in width and all kinds of scraggle and brush has washed up along it.

As I wind around the first part of the bend I see a heap of debris with all sorts of colors. Is this a heap of dead tropical birds or a piled mass of tropical flowers - or both? I pick up the pace and as I near the site my eyes widen and my mouth drops open. What the heck is this? Closer still and it is clear that this mess of debris is neither fowl nor flora. It is a massive array of consumerist cache. I look up and all around, completely stupefied by what I am seeing. Mounds of sneakers, hundreds or perhaps thousands of them - all colors, sizes and styles. All of them Nike. Now I truly feel like Dorothy and the movie has turned to Technicolor.

After so long at sea with only shades of blue and then here on the island just greens and browns added, this mound is a wealth of color. Beyond the sneakers is an enormous deposit of water bottles. Crates and crates of them, strewn about but still intact, glistening in the sunlight like crystals. I peer out at the ocean, staring intently at the water, studying the movement and comparing it with another area further out. What I discern is that the currents converge, circle and do some pretty odd shifting. It seems that the currents around here are favorable to gathering and amassing a lot of flotsam and jetsam, pooling it together and piling it up on this spot.

I kick away a layer of sneakers and underneath I see decayed remnants of I don't know what. All that remains are faded colored bits and pieces of objects that have not degraded and probably never will, yet they are no longer assembled as they once were, their former state no longer discernable.

This is altogether curious but not surprising ultimately. Not long ago, I read that some ten thousand shipping containers go lost every year. Not only that, ten to twelve cargo ships break up and sink every year as well. My island must be situated close enough to these shipping lanes and have strong enough currents to jettison portions of this stuff onto its shore. With all of this stuff piled high in front of me there is only one thing to do.

Go shopping.

Poking and sifting through the sneakers I come across one that looks like my size. Indeed, it is my size and has a nice snug fit. It is blue, which used to be my favorite color before the whole storm, capsize, shark bait, starvation, wash up (and washout) thing.

I kick around and search through more sneakers and find another that looks to be my size. This one is orange and fits snug as well. Fully laced I stand up and try to imagine myself from another's perspective. I can't help but notice that I am wearing a pair of complementary colored sneakers. My gait is now a complementary contrasted rhythm of left and right strides. As I meander along, impressed with my new footwear, I delight in the alternation of colors, the soothing blue and orange beat.

As for the crates of water, I see no use for them. I have no idea how old they are and with the sun beaming down on them day after day the water inside is most certainly contaminated with leached biphenyls and therefore not potable. I could use them to insulate the walls of the hut.

Drinking in the warmth of the sun all day, these bottles would serve nicely as a heat source in the evening. This thought gets stored to the back of my brain for now as the idea of hauling heavy loads of water bottles back to the hut is quite unsavory at this particular instant. Moving further along the heap the inventory shifts to office supplies.

Staples has washed up here and dispensed a boatload (hah) of office scraps. Most of it is damaged by water and insects but there is a lot that has not been breached. Pens, markers, notepads, staplers, and (fuck) paper clips. This, of course, is invaluable stuff and I head inland to get palm leaves to build a sled. I want all of this shit (what is it about office supplies that makes one giddy)?

While gathering palm leaves I consider the best spot for a new shelter. There is no question that I will want to have another base with easy access to CoastCo. With any luck, (or any more fucking incredible luck I should say) Home Depot will wash up some time soon and I can begin work on a respectable shelter, a HippoDome perhaps. I will need some bedding as well. so I will keep an eye out for Bed, Bath and Beyond as I am undoubtedly the Beyond that they are referring to.

It is almost dark. My shelter is built, and I am examining my treasures. I picked out a few more pairs of sneakers for backup. One pair is actually the same color, the rest are unmatched but not necessarily mismatched. On my way back along the heap I found packs of athletic socks.

I made a marvelous mattress and pillow out of them and I lay here astounded by my good fortune. Why are things working out so well for me now? Why are advantages such as these falling into my lap? (a coconut has just fallen beside me - no shit). I guess the divine resonance has considered my shipwreck enough penance and has decided to bestow upon me retched happiness and good fortune.

* * * * * * * * * *

An absolutely divine night rest. Who knew athletic socks were better than Temperpedic? When I am rescued I am going to make mattresses out of these socks. I'll wrap them with a layer of foam and cover it all with an ultra-soft layer of synthetic plushness. Give it an ultra-chic price tag and make a fortune. (This is an altogether fatuous idea. If ever I am rescued and spend the rest of my days making a fortune from this idea, please seek me out and shoot me).

It is unlikely that I will be rescued though. I have been on this island for at least a week and there is no evidence of human presence, now or in the past, as far as I can tell. There is probably a better chance of someone washing up on shore, as I did, than any rescue operation finding me.

Besides, who the hell is looking for me anyway. It has been over a month. No distress signal had been sent and seeing that I contact my friends less than once a month there is no reason for anyone to be looking for me yet. I cast these thoughts aside and stand up to have a look around. What do I need to do today? Expanding the island diet would be a good start. I am growing quite tired of coconuts and crab. Some varieties of grilled fish would do nicely. I decide to take a walk down to CoastCo and see if there is something I might have overlooked that could prove useful for acquiring fresh fish.

At the heap, I kick around for a bit and then I start really digging in. Using some palm sticks and my hands I am able to penetrate deep into the heap (there's that poetry again). Success!!

Lying a few feet below the sneakers are boxes, the insides of which look to be filled with dresses, and indeed they are. It is impossible to read the labels due to decay but the dresses themselves are in pretty good shape so I assume they are cheap, synthetic junk thank God.

I even find some fishnet stockings - shit - not only can I create some kickass fishing gear out of this stuff, I can go fishing in drag. I can transform myself into a gender bending Sea Hag and command the seas! (or the waters just off shore at least).

I traipse back to the shelter and spend the afternoon trying on clothes. I have a delightful time with a number of garment styles and find that dressing in drag is a beautifully liberating experience. I indulge myself with a whole array of roles, from Mae West to Ann Coulter.

What fun! It is so refreshing to be having fun, just playing around for a change. Life should be like this always. I stop and think that perhaps, if people were allowed to play, role switch, and just plain enjoy life we could really get somewhere. It seems to me that this is our evolutionary destiny. Not Trans-Humanism but Trans-Slavery.

The universe is not going to care that we have advanced ourselves with technological, mechanical prowess. It doesn't care if we shoot a rocket over its expanse just to reside there and fuck that area up too. The universe, the resonant energy that is consciousness, is only going to care about us if we demonstrate an ability to resonate with it and add resonant energy to it.

Jean Cocteau once said "God thinks us but does not think of us" It makes sense to me now.

The sole purpose of the Arts and Sciences is to study and connect with our existential experience and bring genuine understanding to our place in the Cosmos and to our role as biological entities intrinsic to this living organism called Earth. Short of that, we remain hostage to our desires and slaves to the desires of others.

Hey, that sounds pretty good. Fresh air and an absence of assholes and morons appears to agree with me. I hardly ever thought much about this stuff before, it was too depressing. Thoughts like these were denigrated and given low priority in the social circles that I navigated. These ruminations were idealistic and naive. Here they are profoundly sensible and obvious. I look back towards CoastCo and remember the water bottles. Fuck yah, let's get those suckers and start sending some notes.

I don an evening gown and hustle down to the heap wishing that I had some elegant heels to go with my outfit. Plenty of time for that later. At the heap, I grab some bottles, open them and dump the water into the ocean. I am concerned that this water may disrupt the ecological balance of the ocean but continue the activity anyway. Maybe the bottled water will affect the fish to such a degree that they will exit the ocean and flop themselves upon the shore where I can scoop them up - another miracle of the fishes?

I return to the Dome and stack a dozen or so empty water bottles in the corner and then shuffle through some dresses, looking for an outfit appropriate for the occasion. Suitably dressed, I head back down to the shore with fishnet stockings and several palm sticks that I can attach to the stockings for leverage. Before long I have a half dozen fish, minnow type dandies that will cook quickly and easily on the fire. I am tempted to take one and bite its head off, separate the eyeballs with my tongue, swirl them around in my mouth and swallow. This does not accord with my new-found lifestyle so I return to the bungalow for a culinary catharsis of cooked fish.

Delectable, the smoky aftertaste sets my memories reeling and suddenly I am remembering all of the places I have been, eating delicious grilled fish. The most memorable, I would have to say, was in Essouira on the coast of Morocco. In the early afternoons, the fishermen would fire up large charcoal pits along the jetties and sell grilled sardines. Wonderfully tasty little fish, the smoky flavor filling one's mouth and permeating the air. Thoroughly satisfied, I recline on my Athletopedic sock bed and reflect.

It is light again, so I suppose that I have slept and have awakened to a new day. Nice to have to surmise such a thing rather than be rudely reminded of it by the by the beeping of an alarm clock. I suppose I should start marking off the days, especially now that I have plenty of paper and pens, but I quickly divorce myself from this thought as I do not want to sustain any habits of my former life that are not useful and tracking the days seems particularly useless to me.

I stretch, yawn, fart and stand up. I have been batting a thousand with my sleep since landing on this island. Never had I such restfulness, such consistency in my life (or what I can remember of my life - I am sure that, as a baby, I slept like this most of the time). I have been full weened off Damitol and feel much better as a result. I no longer desire a neurosis and my health is improving immensely. Today is for writing.

I will start creating bottlepodcasts and get myself out there again. The best way to understand my situation and reincarnation is to write about it, send it off into the ocean of being and assume a presence. I collect all of the writing paraphernalia at my disposal and sit down under the shade of a towering palm tree (yeah, all you writers in the city are so envious, right?) Pen in hand, pad on lap and a coconut by my side I am ready to go.

So, let's go........

OK,now let's go.............................

WTF, get going! Suddenly, I am speechless, or rather writeless. Making a conscious act of this immediately makes it an impossible act. I cannot find any words with which to get started. No problem. I have all the time in the world, so I will sit here until something happens.

* * * * * * * * * *

Well come on Mack - what
about it? Aren't ya even
gonna talk to me?
Mack, what's buggin ya?
For God's sake - say hello
to me.
Oh Mack, you can't act
this way.
I haven't heard a human
voice in four months
Mack   Mack,   say
anything to me, please -
For God's Sake! Talk to
me - say anything

Damn it, I have fallen asleep. Just another movie dream and a blank notepad on my lap. Something new though. My dream, pertinent as all of the others, was in color. This is great. This is portentous for sure. Something is changing. My mind is beginning to alter itself behind my back. This is the thing. Mind does not mind. It tells us nothing of its intentions, it attains its goal and then unveils it after the fact. I cannot see any other way for this to happen, so I accept it and will allow to happen whatever will happen. It is what it is... (similar to I am that I am but without sacred authority).

Mind does not mind....hmm. I write this down on the notepad before I paralyze myself again. I roll up the note, place it into the bottle, add a testicle sized (for lack of a better comparison) rock, cap it and walk down to the water. I stand still for a few minutes and watch the waves as well as the currents farther out. The tide is going out, perfect. I wade out into the ocean until the water reaches my armpits. I reach way back, then pitch my arm forward and cast the bottle out of my hand and into the sea a good fifty feet away. I wait and watch its path through the water. It moves swiftly out and away from the coast and within minutes I can no longer see it.

Godspeed my plastic apostle.

Back at the Dome I prepare some fish. This time with some smashed coconut and salt water for seasoning. I will have to start experimenting with the plant life on the island and determine if there are spice bearing species here. I am content with my menu for now, but I realize that boredom will set in eventually and I will want to expand my diet. I have eaten a bit more than I needed to and elect to go for a walk to spur the digestive juices. I miss my original abode and so head up along the shore and cross over near the tail end of the island then head back down the other side until I arrive at the modest shelter.

Wafts of nostalgia flow through my brain and it feels like I have been away for months. I was a weak and crude human then and so much has changed both in body and spirit. I feel as though the person who built this shelter was an ancestor not me, certainly not the me that I am now. How can this be? Has that much time gone by - weeks, months? I couldn't possibly have lost touch with time to such a degree. Time must be changing. Yes, time is changing. My mind is changing. Time is changing because my mind is changing - or is it the other way around.

Thinking like this is not helpful for me. I have to live in the present - forget the past and give only scraps of thought to the future.

I return to the bungalow and reflect on my excursion to the old shelter. I had checked out the boat to be sure that I had not overlooked anything, which I hadn't. It happened to be high tide. I took advantage of this fact and used a series of logs to roll the boat closer to the water and set it adrift. I pushed it out as far as I could and watched. It was no use, the waves were pushing back towards the shore and before long it was stranded on the beach again. I couldn't rid myself of it and I did not want to go back out there in it either. That notion was not an option for me anymore. No way was I going back out there. I pushed the boat back out as far as I could and came back to shore. Soon the boat was back as well, upright, listing back and forth with the waves. I threw a rock at it and walked away.

The idea of leaving the island has no appeal whatsoever for me. I had been stranded out there for over a month, no one and no thing came close to rescuing me. Why should rescue be a possibility if I go back out there? No, forget it. Not happening. I am glad to be where I am. I collect my notebook and pen and set off again. Providence has set me down in this place and I am staying. Rescue would only be incarceration. That world is gone and so is my enslavement to it. I scribble a note that reflects on these thoughts of rescue then roll up the note with a rock and stuff it inside a bottlepod, toss it out to sea and watch it's movement. I love this moment. I watch the bottlepod cast out to sea and ponder the possibilities.

I shot an arrow into the airIt fell to earth, I know not where

The bottle is off on its own adventure and where it ends up is anyone's guess. Sure, there are mathematicians out there that could figure the probability for where the bottle might or should end up but that's just a logical solution. Imagining where it might end up and who might find it, what it will say to them if anything is the intriguing question. I am fully ensconced in a world of unpredictability here and my mind is changing and morphing in ways I cannot possibly know or anticipate, and this is most stimulating.

I sing in my head a faint and mellow tune from one of Chet Baker's standards –

Imagination is crazy
Your whole perspective gets hazy
Starts you asking a daisy
What to do, what to do

Today I will walk. No, today I will wander. No plans, no goals, no preconceptions about what today should offer. I will wander as a flanuer, casual with no concern for destination. A saunterer of sorts. Thoreau speaks of sauntering in his essay on walking and suggests that the word is derived "from idle people who roved about the country, in the Middle Ages, and asked charity, under pretense of going a' la Sainte Terre, to the Holy Land. The children would see them and yell - there goes a Sainte Terrer, a suanterer.

I am not seeking the Holy Land per se but I have no doubt that these wanderings will take me somewhere - some place in my mind where spirit resides. I head into the interior where wandering is the only way to proceed as the overgrowth forces me to constantly change direction and seek out new avenues. Every so often I stop to examine a plant, inspecting its leaves and putting little bits of it in my mouth. I think about Alexander von Humboldt, his undying enthusiasm for roaming the world and collecting samples of everything he found that had not, to his knowledge, been recorded or examined. What joy, to spend a life discovering and learning about all that exists around you. A world of endless surprise and fascination. For a moment, I am saddened. I think about how much of my world had been mundane and habitual. I think about all of the times that I heard people say that they "hate surprises".
What a strange thing.

I have come upon a plant that appears familiar to me, it looks like it is related to the Aloe plant. The leaves are thick and spongy and ooze an oily whitish fluid when squeezed. The taste is bitter but the feel of it on my fingers is smooth and soothing. I press on and take note of where I am in order to return another time when I am ready to collect samples. The sun is high and sending rays of bright light through the spaces in the canopy above. Beautiful, yellow patches of light dappling over the wealth of green below. I find an area of bright yellow brown and sit for a bit. I look above me and see the pockets of blue sky, radiant against the dark green of the canopy. There are no clouds so the blue is constant, unchanging - caressed by the leaves of the trees. I could stay here all day.

So I stay here all day.

Who knows how much time has passed, I am not bored or hungry so I just sit until the light begins to fade and then head back to the Dome. What a productive day I say to myself (I am speaking out loud to myself and loving it). My mind is in such a good place and I think of how depressed I would be if I was still in my former mind. The idea of accomplishing nothing, at least nothing tangible, would have put me in a bad mood. I think of Thoreau again and recite " a successful man is one who sits along the bank of a river all afternoon and does not feel guilty". That's it. That is what I am experiencing that is so strange to me - a lack of guilt. A care free, free to care less attitude that I embrace "*sans culpabilité*". Why am I using French words these days, I don't even know French?

Let's see…. Crab and fish stew would be nice this evening, but I have no pot to cook stews or soups. I will have to check out CoastCo tomorrow and see if there is anything from Pottery Barn that may have washed up.

Tonight, will have to be smoked fish and crab. Oh yes, wine. Don't forget to look for wine as well. If crates of water bottles can wash ashore, then so can crates of wine - or bourbon for that matter. OK, yes, things are quite nice here thus far but man, some alcohol and a cigar or two would complement all of this beautifully. Civilization does have its good points.

Tomorrow I give some real thought to distillation and/or fermentation possibilities with the plants I have at my disposal. I decide to alternate my days between practical activities and non-practical activities. One day for practical and one day for idle speculation. This approach should serve me well, I think, and seeing as tomorrow warrants practical activity I will begin with the potential for alcohol production (if, in fact, the Heap turns up nothing).

The Heap turned up nothing, so I spent the day looking for berries or any kind of fruit that could serve as an effective source for fermentation with which to poison oneself. One forgets that the effect of alcohol on the senses is a result of poisoning the blood. This does not sound at all appealing or enjoyable, but it is unequivocally both (at least for a good majority of humans).

You may think that spending the day in search of plants/trees suitable for alcohol production is frivolous and of no importance but, in fact, alcohol has been a part of human culture for thousands of years, dating back to the Neolithic period some 10,000 years ago. Some anthropologists/archeologists have even suggested that beer may have preceded bread as a staple of the human diet. There are still doctors in Britain who have no compunction about prescribing a few Guinness stouts to battle a cold as it is high in the vitamin B's. Even though I have not observed much of the island yet, I am quite sure that there is no wheat or barley with which to fashion beer, so I am intent on the distillation process.

Let's not forget the medicinal qualities of alcohol either. Hippocrates (yes, that Hippocrates) created an a somewhat less refined version of vermouth in order to treat intestinal worms.

Distillation spread rapidly with the simultaneous spread of Christianity. Learned from the writings on alchemy and distillation by the Arabs, the crusades brought these ideas and practices to cultures all across Europe. Much of the water back then was badly polluted with disease of all kinds, in particular, Cholera, so drinking various distillations was considered much safer, hence the name "Water of Life".

I am acutely aware of the true water or life, the bottled water that saved my life and the beautifully clear, clean water I have here on the island. Still, I cannot help but think how nice a small, and most likely, crude sample of "Eau de Vie" would be. There has got to be some type of fruit bearing tree on the island. If not, I may have to resort to the old standby – coconuts.

Dusk has arrived more suddenly than expected. Could time be speeding up for me now that I am no longer in a state of suffering and anxiety? I make it back to the Dome and lay back thinking until dream takes over.

＊＊＊＊＊＊＊＊＊＊

Today is a whatever day. I do not have to do anything productive or practical if I don't want to. Actually, I best not phrase it in this way. It doesn't commit me to one option or the other. I should be steadfast and stick to my plan of alternating practical days with days full of idleness and wandering. Saying that I do not have to do anything productive if I don't want to, leaves open the possibility of doing something productive if I want to which is not the same as saying, "I will do nothing practical today". I must be firm about this or I will leave open the opportunity for my former productive/brainwashed self to return. I put on some socks and sneakers and start walking. I begin along the coast because the open sky and hush of the surf seems a good way to start my day. I walk all the way down to the tail end of the island and turn to walk back along the opposite side when suddenly I stall and look up. The BGM is catching the morning's light, reflecting it back with neon- like intensity. Such an odd shape really, or maybe not so odd at that. If I were to associate it with anything I would say it looks a bit like a volcano - a relatively small volcano - kind of like the one I made back in grade school with wire and papier mache'. It has the same funky, lopsided quality my creation had. I decide that it would be a good idea to take a closer look.

I told myself that today was a day for idleness and wandering. Why not wander up to the top of this cone-like enigma and have a look around. From up there I could get a really good sense of the island and its overall topography. I think my sneakers are up for it. I will go back to the Dome and get my machete, finagle something for a walking stick, collect a few feet of rope and set out.

I study the slope and terrain on my way back, looking for any clues as to where I might start climbing. The side that faces out towards the tail of the island is clearly the more accessible, modest slope. There is where I set my sights. The first hundred yards is pretty easy stuff. I am a bit winded, but with just a minute or two of rest I am ready to go again. My curiosity provides me with the energy and incentive to keep moving. Another hundred yards and things are getting pretty tough. It is rockier at this height and therefore less vines to hold on to. I have to use my fingers more and hook them on and into small ridges and crevices and this requires a strength of index I have never to develop and therefore do not possess. My injured hand is surprisingly useful as the thumb, index and middle fingers are what I need most for this climb. I take it slow, really slow, sloth-like, but I'd rather make it to the top than fall to my death. (recall my musings on dying a meaningful death while stranded on the boat)

I come to a significant ledge before long and take advantage of it to rest, have some coconut, and drink some water. I cannot sit but I can lean my body against the rock and stabilize myself with my legs spread and feet turned outward. This allows much relief for my haggard hands and fingers.

From this height things are already looking very different and quite magnificent. The water is a beautiful turquoise color in the shallow regions and the overall shape of the island is a teardrop with a slight curve at the tail as I had surmised when walking around it.

I look up and decide that I can reach the top in two more climb/rest cycles. Plenty of daylight left so I do not feel the need to push myself beyond what I feel capable of. I will have to spend the night up there.

I do not think that I will have the light or the strength to make it back down before nightfall. I am getting use to the semi-nomad lifestyle. Building temporary shelters here and there is a desirable activity and satisfies the architect in me - we are all nomads to some degree, it is in our DNA ; complacency and predictability kills our lust for life (regardless of how often we tell ourselves otherwise), this explains our need to travel, indulge in extreme activities like bungy jumping, parachuting, or shooting ourselves in the head.

My hands and fingers are swollen and bloody but still working. I am one stretch away from the top. I reach and clutch, pull myself up and hump my head and shoulders over the ridge. The next move hustles the rest of my body up onto a level plane of rock and I bring myself to a standing position. I am astonished and nearly fall back but regain my balance and drop my jaw (think rock'em sock'em robots). Below me is a seedbed brimming with life and splendor far beyond what I thought was splendor before this encounter. To my amazement, I am looking down at a volcano. One that has been dormant for quite some time. Everything in the crater is green and thriving with all sorts of vegetation. There is a lake - or what appears to be a lake - in the center, whether it is water or some other concoction of gases and fluids is hard to tell. From here it looks more black than blue but that may be due to the sun being below the volcano's rim at this point.

As much as I would like to venture down there and see what is what, I do not have the strength or enough remaining light to do so. I will use the rest of my energy to prepare a resting place for the night. There are no palm trees up here, so no palm leaves to use. I gather the vegetation in the vicinity, large soft leaves and fern like plants, and pile it all on top of a flat area of rock. This should do. I have no cover or enclosure, but I will have the comfort of the stars as a roof above my head.

The light as faded away, I lie here with only sky above. I am taken back to the nights spent on the drifting hull. My memory of that time is already faint and mixed with good and bad feelings. It is astonishing to think back on how I managed out there. The sea is an awesome power. At first, I was terrified by this power - the great swells and eery silence - but was soon able to cope with it, my fear lost out to the effects of marvel and a surprising peace. This was not a consistent state of mind by any stretch, but it was enough to keep me calm and clear headed and it got me to where I am now.

No dream last night, or maybe I just do not remember. I am surprised that I did not dream. I have dreamt every night for as far back as I can remember and always with a clear and vivid recollection of it in the morning. Is this yet another sign of my changing brain/mind? Perhaps my brain is no longer overtaxed by the burdens of waking life and is choosing to stay silent for a while. I am certainly not alarmed or concerned, nor do I feel the need to overthink this. I let it go and focus on what will be the course of action for today.

I scan the areas to my right and left looking for what might be the best route down to the lake. After a time, it is apparent that one route is as good as another, for everything is subsumed by growth and wild chaotic growth. Being a lefty I choose to descend along the left-hand side with a slow, methodical approach. The overgrowth makes the rock beneath very slippery so I proceed with the utmost caution. Within the first few minutes, I find that scaling down the incline on my side with knees bent and each hand grabbing onto leaves and vines is the most effective technique. Soon I am moving along at a steady pace. Reaching what looks to be the half way point, I stop for a rest and a drink of water. The lake is beautiful in the morning light but with the sun low, as it was when I first viewed it, I cannot tell what it is filled with. The contents will remain a mystery until I can get close enough to examine it with my hands.

There are lots of birds but still no signs of mammal or reptilian life. I am still too far up to see them if they do, in fact, exist. Two more sips of water and I resume my descent. A quarter of the way, I come to a full stop as the growth becomes much thicker and trees are filling the space. The sun is high and it looks to be close to midday. I can see part of the lake through the trees and it is in fact blue which is promising. Although it is slower going now, the trees provide a welcome addition. I can hold on to them at various points along the way and this makes it easier on my legs.

Occasionally I hear rustling that sounds too formidable to be that of a bird. I have yet to see anything other than birds though. There is a clearing about fifty yards or so ahead, off to the right, so I make my way in that direction. I arrive at the clearing and see that it is a stream leading down to the lake. A variety of colorful flowers and birds fill the area and the sound of rushing water, different from the crash of the surf, offers an entirely new and pleasing rhythm.

Further down the stream, on the opposite side, I see an animal. Not very large but definitely a fur topped creature. I step as gingerly as possible, being cautious of any sound my movements may cause. As I draw closer I get a good look at it and as I do I am astounded to see that it is a goat.

A goat?

What the fuck is a goat doing here? As soon as I say this (yes, I do say this out loud, talking to myself out loud has become my new normal) it occurs to me that the goat is looking up, seeing me and probably thinking – "what the fuck is he doing here?"

Now we are both completely still, staring at one another. This continues for some time until my impatience gets the better of me and I take a step closer. Instantly the goat turns and runs back into the thick. Perplexed and steely eyed, I stand still again and think for a bit.

Huh, a goat on an isolated volcano island. Well, so what. There is an explanation for this surely, just as there is an explanation for my being here. Furthermore, I am delighted by the possibility of having milk in my diet again, coconut milk is a poor substitute.

I work my way down along the bank until I reach the spot where the goat was drinking. I see cloven hoof marks in the mud and follow the trail with my eyes until they disappear into the brush. I am not inclined to follow the tracks. I need to rest and think about where I will set up shelter for the night. I begin collecting an assortment of leafy greens in the vicinity and prepare a thick, circular area - circles and spheres being the preferred form of my island architecture style. No enclosure will be needed, I will have the stars above just as the night before. The gentle, gurgling sound of the stream is a welcome accoutrement to my new encampment.

I lay back and clasp my hands behind my head. Staring up at the sky, the light is growing soft, burnishing a rose- colored patina over the clouds hanging low on the horizon. The sound of surging water ripples through the air and soon I drift off into the abyss of light, peace and space.

* * * * * * * * * *

After a short morning hike, I am at the lake. It is not very large and can probably be considered more of a pond than a lake. I think of my visits to Walden pond, in my youth, and this has a striking resemblance to it in size and shape, though everything else in terms of flora and fauna is very different. I reach down and cup a handful of water, it is freshwater with a faint sulphur smell to it. I doubt that it is safe to drink, so I will drink only the water that I brought with me and leave this for future investigation. I do not see any fish, but the water seems to be quite deep and any fish that may be in there are most likely much deeper down. There is a lot of scum collected along the edge and although I have not seen any living creatures I have heard what must be frogs, jumping into the water, always well before I have reached their point of departure.

There are a great variety of birds all around and another dairy delight comes to mind as I gaze up into the trees and notice nests built into the branches on the lower regions which makes climbing and collecting eggs a feasible venture, but I am not the least bit hungry even though it has been some twelve hours since I last ate. Food and drink are rarely on my mind these days. I am fortunate enough to have what my body requires readily at my disposal, so it is no longer a critical concern and therefore my mind wanders elsewhere as my body wanders elsewhere. I am more accustomed to this laissez faire lifestyle than I would ever have imagined prior to my fated voyage. Relieved of the stress of appointments, as well as, traffic and other obstacles to keeping one on schedule, I have a sense of freedom, the like of which I have never known before being washed up on this island. To free oneself, one must cut the bonds of time. I make a note of this for later when I can encapsulate it in a bottelpod and send it off into the ocean.

I have walked the perimeter of the lake/pond and am back at the stream. I head up towards the ridge where I will rest for the night before descending the other side to return to the Dome. The bedding I had prepared two nights ago is still intact and all I need to do is fall back and beam my gaze towards the night sky.

* * * * * * * * * *

Having dosed off for who knows how long, it is very dark, and the sky is populated with so many stars that some areas have the density of clouds. I can see the band of the Milky Way, as well as, clusters and clouds of stars that must be beyond our galaxy - is that possible? I recall being stranded on top of the bottom of my boat and seeing this wondrous sight with the same infinite display of stars, but I view these stars with a different mind-set while lying here on the rim of the volcano. I do not think about what planets I am seeing or the names of the constellations that sparkle throughout the velvet blackness. Naming negates the full range of experience. Looking and observing without naming or categorizing brings another, more actual reality to it all. I am in the moment, seeing how it is rather than what it is. I look more closely and everything expands outward. I feel that I am seeing this expansion, it is stretching outward, gaining in momentum and growing larger by the second. I sense that I am part of this momentum and I find myself completely enveloped by the notion of space and infinity. I am immersed in consciousness itself - not the idea of it or a reflection upon it but the full realm of it - moving outward and onward without direction but always from the center. I begin to feel myself spiraling out and through the darkness punctuated with pings of light and energy. My body becomes charged with a warmth and lightness of being that is achingly unfamiliar. My longing to be has confronted my being as such and the melding of the two comes with a subtle pain that is ultimately benign and passes quickly without diminishing this transformative state.

I awake to a beautiful clear morning and the air has a taste to it that is a bit metallic but is surprisingly appealing. I light breeze comes up off the rim. I experience a kind of weightlessness that isn't levitation exactly but something more akin to what a lesser strength of gravity might entail. I attribute this to a lightness of mind as any other attribution would seem ridiculous. I take up my satchel and prepare for the steep climb down the BGM. I stop half way down for a rest and some water and realize that I am extremely hungry, though nothing can be done about it and I kick myself (literally) for not eating before setting off. I take a moment to imagine eating a morsel of coconut and some leftover crab. This generates some relief and I continue my descent. When I reach the Dome, everything is in disarray but there are no signs of an animal or otherwise and no tracks or markings of any sort.

Strange. Not so strange maybe. This could be the result of strong gusts off the ocean overnight. I scan over everything again then sit down and adjust to being back home. Everything seems different here. I do not feel the need to put things back in their former place. There is an order to it that makes sense and has a balance that is impossible to have imagined prior to my departure.

Upon closer scrutiny, I see that the contents of the Dome are all collected around the perimeter in a circular fashion - even my sock bed has been whorled into a circular form. My mind is quieted in this place and my body seems less real or solid than it did yesterday. I do some stretching exercises in order to reinstate my physical self. As soon as I feel fully corporeal I decide to go off to do some fishing. A dozen or so fish will do nicely and I can spend the afternoon slowly smoking them over the fire.

At the beach-head I see my boat washed up onto the shore and half buried in sand. It looks like some ancient remnant from another world. I look out over the water. The horizon is barely visible because of the haze of humidity hovering out over the sea. I have what I can best describe as a vision while staring out there. Without the horizon, the atmosphere becomes one continuous, expansive volume of space. I am taken back to the neurologist's office where this all began. The corner of the room fluctuating from convex to concave. I sense the energy and vibration that is out there and soon I think I actually see it. A slow, rhythmic whorl of particles all reflecting bright, minute quantas of energy, moving about, enveloping me in its formless radiance. I also become aware of a faint resonance, a low-pitched frequency both inside and outside my head. I stand with the fishing net in my grasp, motionless.

* * * * * * * * * *

It is dark. I have no idea how the darkness arrived or where it came from. Have I been standing here in this spot all this time, hours upon hours? I couldn't have fallen asleep. I am still waist deep in the water, holding the fishing net which is filled with fish. I must be experiencing blackouts - whole chunks of time erased by

some cosmic memory wipe. I attribute the this to a lack of food, telling myself that I have lost consciousness in some way due to low blood pressure and dehydration. The odd thing is that I do not feel weak, not the least bit fatigued or drained in any way. In fact, I am remarkably clear-headed, my legs are not tired, my arms are not tired, but I am much concerned about how and why this is. My senses are having a go with me I think. Perhaps it was close to the end of the day when I came down here, it just didn't register at the time. Maybe I am asleep and I am having a dream within a dream.

The futility of putting any of this together for the purpose of comprehension, settles into my mind and I gather up the net full of fish and head back to the Dome.

I spend the evening hours smoking the fish and mashing up coconut, this will be put aside to ferment. I have acquired a taste for fermented mashed coconut, it does well for balancing my digestion and the sour, tingly sensation is a welcome change from the dullness that derives from a steady diet of smoked fish, crab and raw coconut.

Time for dinner and I am famished. Smoked fish is an appetizing thought after the long hike back from the volcano, the blackout (for who knows how long), and the lack of any real food since yesterday. I fix my gaze on the center of the fire and follow the curling flames upward where they mingle with the sparks. that rise, swirl and fizzle out, trailing off into the night sky to join up with the stars. I think of a stunning series of photos I once saw documenting the Japanese fire festival "Yassai Hossai." It is based on a local legend in which fishermen warm the sea god Ebis, who was believed to have drifted ashore on Ishizu-no-hama beach. In this ancient Shinto festival, three men carry a man in a costume of the sea god and walk through a bonfire, crying "Yassai, hossai." One hundred and eight bundles of wood are burned to ward off evil spirits. The photographs show a fierce fire and as the men carry the effigy through the fire the air fills with sparks that whirl about and bloom into a mass of heat and light that conjures up visions of powerful gods. Sitting before this fire, such visions assert themselves and I sense this powerful God presiding over my inferno.

* * * * * * * * * *

This morning I will walk down the Heap to see if there have

been any new developments there. It has been days (or perhaps weeks) since my last visit so I expect that there will be new shipments waiting inspection. Arriving at the Heap I find all expectations nullified. Upon closer examination, it is clear that not only has there been no new shipments, but a good portion of the Heap has been washed back out to sea.

The same winds that rearranged my lodging also kicked up a surge of surf that swarmed the Heap and took back much of what it had deposited prior to my washing ashore. There were crates of water bottles still clinging to the edge of the shoreline, it being low tide, so I collected a few cases and put them aside. I want to be sure that I have plenty of bottlepods, as I plan on committing myself to a routine of writing and bottlepod casting.

It is important that communications be sent, whether or not they are received is of no consequence. Persistence in this matter is what counts and I am confident that some of what I write will find its way to another sentient life-form somewhere, sometime. I am not doing it with the hope that these bottlepod castings will lead to my rescue. I am simply casting off musings and reflections without information as to who I am or what has happened to me. I am not interested in rescue or hope as it relates to rescue. I only want the act of writing, the making physical that which otherwise exists only in the mind. In fact, with respect to rescue I consider myself rescued, emancipated from what I had not recognized as such but now fully freed of. I have been released of material bonds and superfluous concerns. I have connected to a world- wide web well beyond anything technology could reach. The brain is not the creator of consciousness it is the receptor for consciousness. This is has made itself profoundly clear since my revelation on the rim of the volcano. It is now a matter of opening-up to possibilities, laying waste to presumptions, becoming a quantum being. I have indeed found myself and found my home. I have not been on this island long. A couple of months as best as I can figure. Yet, it might as well be a lifetime. My former life seems like a dream, like one of those old black and white movies I used to dream about. This is what is real, the here and the now. I have never lived so fully in the present as I do now. There is something that happens to the mind once it is recalibrated in this way. I find that the past is no longer past and the future nothing that is ahead of me. Time is all events existing in one time. Perhaps our world is not three dimensional, or four or even ten. It is one dimension, an infinite dimension, stretching out forever in what seems like several dimensions but instead is a fabric of space and time continuously sliding through itself, causing moire'-like interference patterns.

If I should leave this island I am sure that I would die. I do not think that my mind can revert to what it once was, the shock would be too much, my mind would explode, and all would be lost.

You may think that I am indulging myself and not seeing the hard reality, or perhaps telling myself what I want to hear because deep down I fear that rescue shall never happen.

This is normal, faithful reader, you cannot possibly understand where I am now in body and mind. This is not something that can be taught or written about. It is found, and it is found only when one is not looking for it. You may, as I did initially, think that you are setting out to find it. Trailing off to some remote corner of the world in order to resolve that unanswered question.

"Seek and you shall not find".

Just be, in the simplest way possible, and truth will unveil itself.

The World and All That It Implies

Chapter 8   The Discovery: Jacob and Izzy

Jacob

It was already a warm and humid morning, the sun just clearing the tops of the small houses lined along the waterfront leading to the ferry docks. A white, newly painted ferry warmed its engines in the dock far to the left and prepared for the first trip over to the island. This early in the morning only a handful of cars were on board along with a few contractor's trucks, the beach goers would arrive much later.

Jacob looked up when he heard the blast of the motor, the

sound carried effortlessly across the bay to the island shore. He gulped the last sip of coffee, pitched it in the trash and walked onto the beach. He stood for a moment looking out towards the docks across the bay, then steered his gaze over to the left for a second or two before swinging it back and over to the right. Clear skies and a visibility of at least ten miles, this was a fine morning. He looked down at the sand and fixed his eyes on a spot where two foot prints remained from the day before - just two.

He reached into his pocket and pulled out a pack of cigarettes, stuck one in his mouth and stared out over the horizon. He walked back to his truck and pushed in the lighter then walked around to the back of the truck and lifted the metal detector from the back. The lighter popped, he lit his cigarette and returned to the beach.

He loved being out here this early in the morning, knowing he was the first to step onto the beach, like being on the moon. He switched on the unit and turned the gauge three quarters of the way clockwise. He passed it over the two footprints just for the heck of it and, as expected, there was nothing - the unit was quiet. He turned right and walked along the beach twenty yards or so from the water, the unit swaying back and forth in a steady metronome sway over the sand. With his headphones on, the surf was a buffered hiss.

The ocean was of no concern, the vast treasures that may lie at its bottom were of no concern to Jacob. He had no boat, no studied maps telling where sunken treasure might be. His treasures were confined to what lay beneath the sand, much more modest though much more likely to be found. He rarely looked out towards the water while scanning the beach but there was a bright flicker that caught his attention and he looked up and looked hard at what had caused it.

It was a plastic bottle, typical of its kind, but Jacob saw something other than water inside. Probably filled with sand he thought but then, why would it be floating on top of the water, bobbing up and down so spiritedly. He turned off the unit and set it down. The waves were bringing the bottle closer and when he arrived at the edge it was close enough to see that something unusual was inside the bottle. A few more waves rolled in and now the bottle was within reach. Jacob picked it up and saw a small rock and what looked like lined paper neatly rolled up. He stared at it a moment then looked up and out towards the horizon.

A fucking message in a bottle - really?

It must be some kind of prank he thought. A message in a plastic water bottle seemed hardly authentic. What he meant by authentic he didn't know but something wasn't right.

He walked back to the truck staring at the bottle and moving it around in his hand. It was completely dry inside. Somebody must have thrown this in the water last night for a lark. Probably the same person who left the two footprints in the sand. He pulled the tailgate of the truck down and leaned forward resting his elbows on the back and studied the bottle, turning it over and rotating it one revolution at a time. He put it down and walked over to the passenger side of the truck, opened the door then the glove compartment and grabbed the pocket knife inside. Back behind the truck he picked up the bottle and sliced off the top just below the neck where the circumference was largest. He dumped out the rock and out fell the paper still rolled up, concealing any writing or drawing that may be on it. He carefully unrolled the paper and saw that there was indeed writing.

"Mind does not mind. It tells us nothing of its intentions,

it attains its goal and then unveils it to one after the fact."

What the fff.... some stoners must have written this down and stuck it in the bottle for the hell of it. He didn't see much sense in the writing. It reminded him of some the stuff he read in a philosophy class he took as an elective some years ago. Messy, heady stuff that wasn't going to get him a job.

He got in the truck and headed home. There was something about this message in a bottle that worked on him. No other thoughts were going to divert it. This was a new and puzzling experience and Jacob had not had an experience quite like it that he could remember. The more he thought of it the less it seemed like a prank. He had spent years combing the beach and never came across anything like this. He saw plenty of writing in the sand over the years. The typical night nellers writing their name or their lover's name or just saying Hello. He wondered if there was something more to read into this, or was it just some chance occurrence without any meaning at all. Life oscillates between random and planned events, this is nothing more than a random event. But why him? If he had not noticed the glint off the bottle out there in a sea full of glints he would have kept moving on down the beach with his head in the sand. And why wasn't it a plea for help or something like that? Why this cryptic message? Who would bother to write an arcane message like this and stick it in a bottle? A rock was added for ballast so there was no doubt about intention, it was intended to reach somewhere and somebody.

He was so caught up in these thoughts that he drove straight past his driveway and so decided to continue downtown and get

146

a coffee. Rachel, who owned the shop, handed him his coffee. He told her about his find and pulled out the note so that she could read it.

"Hmm.. That's weird - some beach bard probably."

"Yah, something" said Jacob then headed out to the truck and drove home.

Jacob sat down at his computer and checked his messages. The usual stuff, nothing to save or respond to - not now anyway. He stretched back in the chair and took a deep breath, exhaled with a sigh and stared at the screen. He looked over all of the familiar icons that covered the screen and the others down below on the dock. A couple of notifications on Twitter and Facebook but nothing on Instagram. He placed the note on the table and photographed it with his phone. He opened up Twitter and typed out the message beneath the picture of the note along with the caption "Found this in a bottle washed up on the beach this morning - Fucked up, yah?"

He did the same for Facebook and Instagram then put the computer to sleep and went into the kitchen for something to eat.

* * * * * * * * * *

Izzy

Izzy combed is beard and drew the end to a point, brushed back his shoulder length hair and tied it in a ponytail. One last look in the mirror and then out to the porch where his bike was leaning against the railing.

He rode along the dirt road to an intersection where he turned east and headed down the two-lane highway toward Bingham Bay. It was slightly over-cast and the air had moisture lingering like a light sweat. Izzy locked his bike to the railing of the boardwalk and walked down to the water and out onto the jetty. He walked to the end and sat down crossed legged with arms resting on his knees and hands in the gyan mudra position. Waves crashed upon the rocks of the jetty creating a steady rhythm that filled the space around Izzy and set the stage for his descent into a deep meditative state. His breathing in and out synched with the movement of the water.

Most mornings began in this way. Izzy was always surprised and grateful that no one else was ever here when he arrived. It was early, but it was the perfect time for anyone looking for a peaceful spot to relax by the water yet, each morning, Izzy was the only person sitting upon the rocks. Rising gently out of his meditative state, Izzy opened his eyes and peered out over ocean. It was clear and bright, the sun well above the horizon now with no clouds in sight. He looked down where the water was slapping against the jetty and saw a plastic bottle bobbing up and down between two large rocks.

"Damn it, those fuckers are everywhere."

Izzy climbed down to the edge and retrieved the bottle. He was startled to see that the bottle contained something other than water or air. It had a small rock and a piece of paper in it. He uncapped the bottle and stuck his index finger in as far as it would go down through the space in the center of the curled paper. Pressing his finger against the side of the bottle, the paper cinched between, he carefully rotated the bottle which rotated the paper until it was rolled up tight around his finger. He slowly pulled his finger and the paper up and out of the bottle. He rolled out the paper and read what was written.

"I stare into the void and the void stares back"

Izzy stood dumbfounded and thought to himself. This is incredible. This is precisely what I have been trying to articulate to myself each time I meditate. I have seen this void and realized its presence. Now I am touching it. This is a sign, a connection to that void and it is not only staring back it is talking back (or at least writing back). This cannot be an accident, it is not some random

149

event that I have happened upon. It is I who, of all the oceans of the world and of all the people of the world, has come upon this bottle and this message, here in this place and time.

Izzy was awed, his head overwhelmed with a myriad of thoughts that steered his mind towards an ecstasy he had wanted for all his life. Here was verification of a higher consciousness, a validation of his connection to it. He had been looking, waiting for just this kind of sign. It was no surprise to him that it would find him in this way. He has been coming to this spot every morning since he cleaned himself up and rid himself of addiction. His mind has been clear for months and all sorts of realizations and connections had been building, culminating on this day, with this event.

He tucked the note in his breast pocket and walked back to his bicycle. Riding back a thousand thoughts passed through his mind, tumbling over one another and folding into themselves. He barely felt his physical self at this point. The ride home was automatic and streamed past unrecorded, leaving no imprint, no memory. All that registered was light and impulses, high energy frequencies that left Izzy speechless and confounded, with an excitement that rattled his nerves and diverted his attention from all that lay outside his mind.

It was dark and the evening was alive in the twilight. Izzy

opened his eyes and looked out over the water. How is it he was here on the jetty again? Where did all the time go and how much time? Is it evening of the same day or that of another day? He felt inside his breast pocket, the note was still in there. He peered down along the edge of the jetty. He didn't really think that another bottle would be found there but nothing seemed impossible anymore. In fact, it was impossible to think that this note was the end of it. He looked back and saw his bike. So, he did ride here. Or did he ever leave? He had no memory of what had transpired, just the memory of finding the note and a vague notion that time had passed. He pulled out the note and read it again.

"I stare into the void and the void stares back"

Shit!

* * * * * * * * * *

Jacob

Jacob woke to the rizzing of a leaf blower rolling back the blanket of leaves on the neighbor's lawn. Nine o'clock. His alarm would go off soon anyway, so he lay there waiting for it.

Today was not a beach-combing day, it was a day to sleep in.

151

He rose and stretched, headed to the bathroom and then the kitchen. A cup of coffee in hand, he sat down and woke up the computer. Glancing at the desktop he was stunned to see that there were hundreds of Facebook and Twitter responses. He opened both and started reading. Some were from friends saying that they saw his post and thought it "really fucking cool" or they thought he was "full of shit". Then there were the responses from those whom he did not know. People who found his post "amazing" and others expressing their wish to have found something like this themselves. Then came the truly astounding responses. People who had come across posts similar to his. Other messages had been posted giving accounts of messages found in a bottle all over the country and overseas as well. They posted links to these postings and Jacob read each one. He spent the entire morning reading all the posts and links to other posts. One person had set up a page putting all the messages found so far onto it. He said that he was writing a book about this "strange series of events that had occurred all across the globe."

Jacob picked up the message still laying there beside the keyboard and read it. Then he read all of the other messages that he saved from the web. Was this one person? Maybe there was a group of people doing this, trying to inspire some sort of collective conscience in order to wake us up. He figured that it was more likely that someone threw a bottle in the ocean as a lark and then once it was found and reported, others followed suit. This is the kind of mob activity that flourishes on social media. It is fun to be part of it, but it is also annoying to think that one is being fucked with. He put the computer to sleep and went to get dressed.

* * * * * * * * * *

Izzy

Izzy wandered back to where he had left his bicycle, hopped on and rode back home. Inside everything looked different. Not new or even strange but oddly detached from any memory stored in his head. It was his home, no doubt about that, but it was out of sorts - not in a disorganized way, it was more of the meaning and attachment to the objects that was different - he had no sense that these things belonged to him. This dissolving of material attachment gave Izzy comfort and he saw relationships between these objects rather than simply seeing and identifying them. Colors and patterns presented themselves. Textures were amplified by the light and clarity of his perception. He felt these things through his vision and it generated a fortifying dynamic that coursed through his mind and body. Everything was alive, energy emanating from all sides. Why was this a calming atmosphere instead of a manic one? Why was this influx of energy from every object not overwhelming him?

He sat down finally and gazed up at the blank ceiling - swirls and patterns developed and then tiny dots blinked on and off. The ceiling receded into a vast, boundless space. The silence was restorative. His stomach suddenly whined and then growled, he realized that it had been hours, perhaps days, since he ate last but until now he had not noticed. He fixed some pasta and a salad and as he ate he noticed a profound change in the taste of everything. Flavors were more intense, subtle nuances of salty and acidic combinations, varieties of delicate spices played across his palate. The acuteness of all of his senses was exciting, invigorating. What had brought this on was still unclear, but Izzy was certain that this was the turning point that he had been searching for. The note was merely the catalyst, the physical signal to all that lay unspoken.

"I stared into the void and the void stared back"

The void was staring back, and Izzy was taken with the immensity of it, the prodigious void that encompassed all and nothing. Understanding without trying to understand, knowing all that cannot be known. This was ecstasy, this was the absolute center of everything. Frequency, resonance, balance of polarities - all that exists and all that has existed rolled into one dimension, one reality that reveals all reality.

The next morning Izzy sat in the kitchen, tapping his fingers on the table and shaking his head with quick quirks. He listened closely to the ambient sounds around him. The tick of the clock, the hum of the refrigerator, car doors slamming closed outside on the street, high and low-pitched shouts. There was a harmony to all of this – fixed but impermanent. All aspects of Izzy's surroundings were penetrating and calibrating their presence within him.

This was new, really new. Although Izzy was astonished by each new event and perception, he was not disoriented in the least. In fact, his thinking was clear and focused. He had a plan and he was ready to implement it this very day. He went into the bedroom and packed a small duffle bag with a change clothes and an extra pair of sneakers. He brought his bike inside and parked it in the living room. Outside he locked the door behind him and set off on foot towards Bingham Bay, stopping first at the corner market to pick up some bottled water and light snacks.

Arriving at the Bay and looking down along the coastline he decided to head south. It was a jagged, rocky coastline but it was easy to navigate, at least along this particular section. Izzy enjoyed the challenge of finding the best path or line to take along the irregular contours of the rocks. Still more challenging was keeping an eye on the water's edge while navigating among the rocks. Izzy was on a quest to find more bottles. He was sure that there were more out there and that he was destined to find them and bring continuity to this mystery of the message.

When he got to the next town he walked inland along the boulevard where a variety of seaside shops were located, each bringing color and character to the sun scorched town. Izzy went into a small shop mid-way on the boulevard, one of the oldest shops that specialized in memorabilia and maritime artifacts. He was looking for a pair of binoculars and there on the front table were a pair of cruise ship binoculars. The price was modest, and they were small enough not to be an encumbrance to him on what was sure to be a long excursion. The elderly woman was reading a book and looked up once she noticed Izzy had stopped in front of her, having found something of interest. She squinted and noticed Izzy was holding the pair of binoculars. She asked if he was going on a cruise to which Izzy replied that a cruise was not in his plans but a long journey down the coast was and did she by any chance know the weather forecast for the week. Older folk always know the weather. Not that it is sure to be accurate, but it is sure to be relayed, to anyone listening, as detailed and accurate. Izzy considered the weather prediction of the woman and decided to stop in the

Sun'N'Beach shop down the way and pick up a plastic poncho.

* * * * * * * * * *

Jacob

Jacob slipped on his sandals and went out to the truck. He was hungry so he went downtown to the coffee shop to sit and talk with some of the locals about what he had found and what was revealed after posting it on the social media sites.

"Some fuckers just hav'in some fun, that's what I say"

This came from Don who had been born and raised in the area and was the sort to take everything at face value and not worry about the particulars.

"Ya, that's what I thought", said Jacob, "These kids today are all about spectacle and bringing attention to themselves."

"If someone was gonna bother to put a note in a damn bottle it would be for help, not some cockamamie philosophical crap" Don added.

Jacob stirred his coffee and took up a piece of bacon and

chewed it while staring outside where a group of pigeons were fighting over some scraps beside the dumpster. Jacob exhibited indifference about the matter, but underneath it all he felt there was something more to the circumstances surrounding the messages washing up along the coast and elsewhere. He had lived on or near the water his whole life and nothing like this had ever occurred. Then again, things just happen sometimes, all the time in fact, getting stranger and more unpredictable with every turn. Why shouldn't something like this happen, he thought. Life is stranger than fiction, this has been proven many times over. What about the time on the beach three years ago? He was combing the coast and the meter spiked, something significant was there. He dug down in the sand and found a locket with his picture in it. It was Shannon's locket. She had lost it while swimming a year before their breakup. Jacob remembered thinking that she had not lost the locket after all but had buried it there in the sand after an argument, the one that led to their finally ending the relationship. If Shannon had buried it then the find was not so strange, but if she hadn't buried it well, that was kind of strange but not all that extraordinary. Still, he couldn't bring himself to believe that anything other than chance and randomness was responsible for the note.

* * * * * * * * * *

Izzy

Izzy left the shop and returned to the coast to resume his journey south. By mid-day he was a couple of miles down the coast. Here the rocks receded farther back from the water and there was more, sandy beachfront. The sun was high now and it was burning through his hat and heating his head to an uncomfortable temperature. He stripped down to his shorts and ran into the water, diving under as soon as he got waist high. He swam for only a minute or so and then was back out putting his shirt and sneakers on. He turned and looked back out towards the horizon and scanned across from left to right watching for any anomaly that might present itself on the surface of the water. Nothing.

He walked back onto the sand and sat down to rest. He got a granola bar and bottle of water from his pack and ate while considering his plan. He would continue walking until sunset and stop for dinner in whatever town was within reach at that point, then head back to the beach and set up the tent for the night. He could probably cover a good fifteen miles or more by sunset and that should bring him close to Whipsalem. He had been there just once but remembered a simple diner right in the center of town that would do nicely for dinner.

That settled, he stood up, slung his gear over his shoulder and started down the coast. The sun flaunted its heat, drying Izzy's clothes within the first mile. He was not much bothered by the heat and he found that he was in a state of mind congruent with that he had experienced while meditating on the jetty. The steps were easy and repetitive now that the rocky coast had given way to sand, the rhythm was a basic four over four measure, and his breathing complemented this by an inhale and exhale hitting on every other beat. This set up a pleasant pace that inspired rumination and reflection which guided Izzy into a variety of complex thoughts and connections. Why is there something rather than nothing? Why is the Earth mostly water when the moon is just a dry dusty rock and all the other planets are hot, molten spheres or whirling masses of gas? Even if this is the result of wild chemistry and fruitful biology, how the hell did it all begin?

Izzy thought about his life and how it seems to have had just as mysterious a beginning, particularly since finding the message. Up until that point, he was living and, so he thought, searching for meaning in his life. He thought back to when he was a student and had taken an art history course as an elective. Art was a keen interest of his although he had no capacity for expressing himself in any of the creative disciplines, or any disciplines for that matter. This was the problem he grappled with all his life. The professor was an accomplished lecturer and brought up various quotes of artists to drive home a particular point relative to the creative process. One of the quotes that had always stuck with him was from Picasso - "I do not seek, I find". It had the token bravado of Picasso, but it was the conviction of finding that nestled in Izzy's mind. One can search and search, move from one teacher or mentor to another, continue to ask questions and seek an answer but one must settle the matter finally and take a direction, commit to a point of view and then do one's best to destroy that point of view or decide that this view has depth and breadth for further discovery. Izzy then recalled a statement of Mondrian who, speaking of what he desired from the act of painting, said something to the effect of "I am not interested in making pictures, I just want to find things out".

Izzy had wanted to "find things out" as well but had no recourse for doing so. His search turned inward and wallowed in the blurred, inchoate realm of the subconscious. Finding the message in a bottle, a startlingly prescient message, had opened new vistas for finding a direction in his life. He had found rather than searched this time and he was sure that this event was a turning point, he felt it deep down where thought does not reside, and doubt has no meaning. This message was clear as the sand in front of him, granular and consistent, like time. He was walking the coastline, for how long did not matter, for what reason did not matter, the walk itself would reveal the nature of it and lead to what would come next. He knew that this trek was not really about finding more bottles with messages. This was unlikely when one considered the odds, it was more to do with separating from the ordinary and casting himself a wider net with which to capture the truth of what life was all about.

* * * * * * * * *

Jacob

Today was a beach combing day. Jacob rose earlier than usual and had spent close to three hours scanning and digging. Not a particularly productive day, a few coins, a watch and a thin gold necklace with a small gold beach ball. Most of what Jacob found was worthless stuff like this but he saved all of it and a couple of times a month, at most, he would take it over to Jedd who owned a small pawn shop just off the main street in the center of town. He was planning on heading there at the end of the week.

Jacob returned home. It was hot inside, the sun was breathing heavy now and the shingles absorbed the heat and radiated it throughout the house. He turned on the fan and sat down at the computer. As he suspected, there were more Facebook and Twitter posts commenting on his find, as well as, other posts providing links to some of the messages found in the last few months, some of which he had already seen but a few new messages as well. This was clearly turning into a fad he thought, it was sure to wear thin as some other event or oddity would come along to replace it. He saw that he had a message in his personal mailbox and clicked it open. "Hi, you do not know me, but I have come across your posts on Facebook and Twitter and I am very much interested in the message that you found. I have been following all the other posts about messages found in bottles and I am planning on writing a book about it. I would very much like to buy your message from you if you would be inclined to sell it. If so, please respond and we can talk over the details.

Thanks Seth"

Buy my message? That seems a bit strange, I mean, how does he know if my message is even authentic. What does it mean to call it authentic anyway – it's just a prank. Jacob sat back in his chair staring blankly at the screen, thinking about what this Seth guy could possibly be up to. Obviously, an opportunist/writer hack, looking to cash in on this fleeting folly. I wonder how much he would be willing to pay? he thought out loud.

He decided that he would write back, feel him out and see what kind of price this guy would be willing to put on his message. He was beginning to feel as though the whole thing was moving beyond him. Why would someone want to buy his message? Why hadn't he considered it a valued commodity when he found it? Does he even consider it to be one now? Not really. He was convinced that this was all a meaningless farce, something generated out of boredom or caprice. He could not apply any real importance to it, nor did he want to. He would sell the damn message and be done with it.

He went into the kitchen and checked the fridge. All the stuff that was in there last night was still there this morning. He scanned the collection while filtering through a jumble of thoughts bouncing around in his head, his eyes turned inward, glazing over the contents of the fridge. After a few minutes, his eyes alighted on the bacon pushed all the way towards the back. He took half of it and placed it in a pan.

While the bacon sputtered and hissed, Jacob's thoughts ran backwards and forwards until a loud spirt broke the rhythm and he saw that the bacon was ready. A ding from the toaster signaled the completion of the toast and the eggs were nonexistent so breakfast was ready.

He brought his meal over to the computer, sat down and hit the space bar to wake it up. He trolled through his emails and discarded all the petitions, appeals and sales pitches, read a few of the top news stories, then logged into his Facebook account.

He had many new notifications, all of them still addressing his message in the bottle and offering up a variety of theories as to what it signified. There was another inquiry from the writer asking him if he had decided whether he was going to sell his message or not. Jacob sat back in his chair and crunched his toast while gazing up at the ceiling. There was a small bug crawling across the center and he could not tell if it was a spider or some tiny insect. Either way, he was impressed with its ability to wander upside down up there, effortlessly and without risk. He thought of what it might be like to be able to do that himself. He imagined wandering upside down along the ceiling of an office or department store, as natural as anything else he did every day, then strolling down the wall back to an upright position on the floor. How cool would that be to experience three-dimensional space so completely, without the limits imposed by gravity.

The computer dinged with the arrival of a new message and Jacob peered down at the screen to see what had transpired. It was one of his virtual friends asking him if he had heard about the guy who had also found a message in a bottle and had become a sort of an evangelical preacher, drawing large crowds at a city park and inspiring a wave of optimism about the messages. He believed the messages were the work of a messiah living in some remote corner of the world and relaying his epiphanies through bottled words - he called himself Ultramarine. Jacob chuckled to himself and folded his arms as he sat back again in the chair.

A fuck'in messiah - are you kidding me?

In that case, I had better hang onto my message - frame it even. He laughed again, got up and took his empty plate back to the kitchen.

A messiah? In this day and age?

He shook his head and walked back to the computer to put some music on. He thought about playing Handel but decided that it would only make him want to lay back and go to sleep so he played some Radiohead instead. He went back to his thoughts about being an insect and walking all around the room. This brought him to thoughts about Kafka and he wondered if his story was prompted by drifting thoughts he had while watching a cockroach amble about in his dingy flat. Why the heck would anyone be moved to write a story about waking up as a cockroach - damned nasty things. He entertained the idea of writing a story, not about the bottled message as that hack was doing, but something more to do with a spider and its view of the world. Spiders, he thought, must have some level of aesthetic about them, their webs are visual as well as engineering masterpieces. They don't just make them that way for no reason, otherwise, why wouldn't they construct a simple and straightforward grid to catch their prey? No, there was intelligent design involved here. More intelligent than what was being conveyed in any of these messages washing up all over the coast, that's for sure. Some chuckleheads out there are certainly having a good laugh for themselves. If they have any intelligence at all they will step it up and start making a concerted effort to direct the dialogue towards something tangible, perhaps lead it all towards unmistakable evidence of alien life infiltrating our planet.

Now that is something I could get behind thought Jacob. He had always been fascinated by the prospect of alien life forms and the possibility that they could already be here among us. He had heard a recording on the internet years ago, talking about aliens coming to earth in the form of reptiles, way back in Sumerian times. They landed in what became known as the Garden of Eden. They made many attempts to breed with human beings, but the offspring had always aborted. After two thousand years, the offspring started to take, and the reptile aliens were able to multiply and live as shape shifters on the planet and they are here with us today, most of them in positions of power. Jacob was intrigued by this story and spent several months investigating the evidence, of which there was none, and became fascinated by the idea that this could be and perhaps was the case. Aliens had populated the planet and were living here completely anonymous, exploiting all of us with their cleverness and superior intelligence. They don't write stupid notes and send them out into the ocean inside a plastic water bottle - shit. Just the same, he was going to hold onto his message and keep it safe for now

The World and All That It Implies

Chapter 9   **The Revelation**

Dark, rumbling, cumulonimbus clouds were bunched along the horizon like a heavy rope. Izzy looked out from his tent and assessed the potential for serious weather. It was high tide and he was worried about a storm surge in the middle of the night that could wash his tent and supplies away. So far, things seemed relatively calm, the clouds far out at sea and uninterested in moving inland. There were still stars directly overhead and this was a good sign in Izzy's mind. He laid back down and listened to the distant thunder.

Funny, he thought, that thunder could be a comforting sound, the low- pitched mumblings of tired Gods. He fell off into a semi-conscious state and then slipped into a dream.   Faces streamed in and out of view and voices spoke to him. These images and sounds morphed into patterns then crystalized into colors. Whirling about, the colors seized his whole being and lifted him up into a cloud of noxious matter and dizzying delights - the contrasting blend confusing his senses. The middle of this mix gradually opened from the center and a radiant light shone through striking Izzy squarely on the head and, startled out of restfulness, he jumped up and threw open the flap of the tent.

The clouds were up on the beach now and reaching down with dark tails sparked with lightning. A blast of brackish ocean air filled the tent and it began to lift from the sand. Izzy grabbed the tubular supports and held on. Lightening cracked overhead and boomed inside his chest, leaving ripples in the sand around his feet. Rain lashed his face and stung his eyes, he felt as if he could drown standing up. Another bolt of lightning and belt of thunder and Izzy fell to his knees, still clutching the tent supports and bowing his head away from the torrents of rain and wind.

"I know" he screamed. "and you know I know."
He stood up again and released the tent which careened up into the air and out of sight. He saw his pack on the sand and dove down on

top of it. Water rushed over him, flowed back and left him shivering there on the sand. The wind receded as well, and the sky rapidly cleared overhead letting the light of the moon shine down on and around Izzy's stunned silence.

He got to his feet, gazed up at the moon and shook like a dog. "I've got to get home"

A couple of overnights in chemically bathed motel rooms and Izzy was back home, the events of his journey still resonating in his head. He had a call from a friend inquiring as to his whereabouts and if he had heard about the messages found inside plastic water bottles washing up all over the coast - cryptic, philosophical kinds of notes that sound like something Izzy would have written if he were stranded on an island somewhere.

" WTF eh Izzy?"

This did not surprise Izzy so much as confirm a feeling he harbored ever since finding his message. Of course, there are other messages washing up. This is a communication for those ready to listen - ready to switch off their phones, squelch their distractions and deliver themselves from solipsism. The tide had turned and he was prepared to harness this wave of consciousness and bring it to the masses. His meditation had drawn this message to him and perhaps to others who were ready to receive.

Dan Shore, his friend, had called because he knew it was something Izzy would recognize as significant, not arbitrary. Dan Shore. Of course, Dan Shore knew who to call, no question. He would call him back and ask that he send him all the messages that had been discovered thus far.

* * * * * * * * * *

It was two o'clock in the morning and Izzy was writing wildly, full of feverish energy that only words could complete. Dan had sent twenty-two messages already and Izzy saw the connection instantly. There was an odd coherence to all of the messages. When read together they communicated a frame of mind that did not sound like ideas generated from a variety of different people from different places, nor anything produced by random acts of tomfoolery.

No, these messages were from one mind, one entity that found a resonance in the atmosphere and mingled this with the isolation emanating from the muddled communications pouring out of the digital cloud of forgetting. This entity was a person, one of this Earth but distanced somehow, remote from the world and all that it implies but undoubtedly a product of it. All twenty-two messages were truths that philosophers of all the ages have pondered and struggled to understand. Here were the words and works of a generous mind, one that has found wisdom in nature and in silence. The notes arrive silent, hermetic, out of time and place, enigmas enclosed in a skin of perfect, impermeable polymer, clear and colorless but for the colors it reflects.

It was all coming together, forming a picture of what had to be, what was going to be, forever. Izzy was never more sure of his thoughts and he could see the future as clear as he could see the clock on the wall. It was laid out before him like a scroll, rolling out in perfect synch with the thoughts coursing through his mind. If there was ever a time for action, Izzy thought, it is now. The signs were all there, his focus and concentration primed and poised, his mind empty but for this one purpose. He still felt the heightened sense of awareness that overtook him the morning of the sojourn down the coast. Colors were vivid and nuanced, subtle shifts towards red or violet were easily discernable, the contrast of cool and warm tones created a balanced field of light that created energy all around him. Touch was electric, vibrations fast and penetrating, he could sense objects as cymatic patterns, beautiful arrays of concentric rings and loops formed his perceptions.

He looked over at the book shelf, the space in the middle

where no books resided, a simple wood carved figurine of Jesus about a foot high. Izzy had found it many years ago in a second-hand shop, an exquisite balance of crudity and craftsmanship, an aesthetic perfection impossible to achieve through technique alone. This humble statue conveyed suffering, humility, human-ness and grace that was more genuine to him than many of the great masters like Michelangelo. This was created by someone without pride or want for artistic greatness, monetary compensation or immortality. It was a product of love, a love that had no other intentions. Izzy adored the rugged Jesus, as he liked to call it, the very sight of it now touched his heart and provoked his psyche. He thought about the message he had found, as well as, the messages others had found, they had the same genuine sensibility and intent that the rugged Jesus had - of this he had no doubt. The signs and sensations were true and unmistakable.

Next morning Izzy set out for Thompson Square Park, a small, quaint, but not well-kept area nestled between two colleges, notorious as a place for the marginalized factions of people both young and old to congregate, air their grievances, perform tricks (the circus type) or play hours of chess and backgammon. Modest crowds would often gather during the lunch hour and on weekends, curious types seeking conspicuous, peculiar, or utterly wacky expressions of life out of balance.

Izzy set up a music stand and perched his notebook on it. He opened a plastic bag full of flowers he had picked from the gushing gardens surrounding the corporate building a couple of blocks away from the park. There were areas on both sides of the building, blocked from the view of the main entrance and, for special occasions, Izzy would extract a few flowers. He told himself that this was a service to the flowers which went unnoticed and unappreciated otherwise. Today was more than a special occasion, so he had bagged a copious collection of flowers and spread them out all around the base of the music stand. Leaning against the front of the stand he placed a sign he had made - "Ultramarine" - painted with blue acrylic paint. The ultramarine pigment was originally created by grinding Lapis Lazuli, a semi-precious stone found in Afghanistan, into a powder and mixing it with linseed oil to bind it into a buttery consistency. It was an expensive pigment when it was first produced hundreds of years ago, and much sought after by artists all across Europe. Because it came from so far away it was named ultramarine - "across the sea" - therefore Izzy thought this to be a particularly apt name - it suited his identity.

Dressed in blue jeans, a white mandarin collared shirt with a blue handkerchief in the breast pocket, and brown shoes, Izzy positioned himself behind the music stand, grunted a few times, coughed, shook out his arms and stood erect with his chin slightly raised, his eyes wide open staring upwards toward the sky. Breathing in deep, he bellowed –

"I stare at the void and the void stares back"

A couple of people turned their heads as they walked by and others sitting nearby looked directly at Izzy with more of an irritated look than anything else. Izzy spoke the words again, this time a bit softer than before and with a slower delivery and an emphasis on "stare" and "stares".

When finished, he looked to both sides and then out towards the people walking, standing and sitting. "These words came to me from across the sea, in a bottle made for holding water but instead contained a piece of paper, a scroll if you will, imparting this message. A message about the void, a message coming out of the void itself and into the realm of the living. This was not the only message, many more would follow, washing up upon shores all over the planet. I bear witness, we all bear witness, to this extraordinary phenomena as it unfolds in our midst. I am compelled to ask – Why?

Why this particular message, and why now? What is one to make of all the other messages rescued from the abyss? All of you must ask this question as well. For whom are these messages intended and for what possible reason? But reason does not play into this, at least, not reason as such. I believe we have been summoned, summoned to acknowledge the voice from without in order to acknowledge the voice from within, but we have lost our capacity to listen to the voice within. We suffer the indifference of the universe and recoil from that which we do not know or understand."

Izzy's voice was confident yet gentle, it pierced the skin of stifling noises surrounding the park and spread out in all directions. Some of the people seated nearby put down their phones, others approaching from both directions slowed their pace and gave each other puzzled looks. Some stopped abruptly and considered the situation as though there might be repercussions to follow. Izzy, sensing that he was getting through, started up again with more verve in his voice and making eye contact with those who were within sight.

"Mind does not mind - it tells us nothing of its intentions, it attains its goal and then unveils it to one after the fact."

This curled some eyebrows and drowned out a nearby sneeze. People began conversing with one another about what was going on here, chuckling in disbelief and rolling their eyes. Someone said it must be Sunday and strolled off with their hands pressed together. Two teenage romancers sitting on the bench to the right of Izzy peered up from their embrace and hollered "Fuck'in right" while giving him a thumbs up.

"We speak of free will but can any of us really say that we are acting freely? How many constraints hold us to inaction or indifference? Do we even recognize these constraints? Is mind in us or out there somewhere tapping on our heads from time to time? Have any of you even thought about this recently, or at all?
Idle hands are not the devil's workshop – it is idle minds, distracted minds, minds full of busy-ness.

These messages, coming from the sea, are an opportunity, a chance to wake from our sleep and confront the real, even the unimaginable. We, every one of us, are intelligent, empowered beings who have been systematically marginalized. We are box bred and box fed, then told to think outside of this box, all the while knowing that what lies outside the box is a bigger box.
Fuck the box!"

Izzy caught himself and stopped. He did not want to engage in profanity not to mention the sexual connotation it relayed. "You might think this, but it is not getting outside of the box that is the problem – it is negating the existence, the very idea and acknowledgement of the box that is the goal.

A small crowd was now forming. Izzy ended his incantation

and looked around, until now he was completely unaware of this transformation. A veritable throng had developed, and Izzy was imbued with a prodigious energy and keen sensation. He was larger than he had ever been before, his lungs expanding and craving oxygen. At the same time, a wisp of calm curled around him, enveloping his thoughts so that he no longer felt the need to speak. He simply looked out at the crowd and, one by one, espied the emptiness and the yearning, grasped the wanting expressions and sponged them with his vision. A silence prevailed for several minutes.

Nothing seemed to move, although the rest of the city was immersed in the usual chaos. Izzy continued until he hit upon every eye that presented itself to him. Then he stepped back, closed his notebook, knelt down in front of the music, plucked a flower from the pile and handed it to the nearest person. The crowd encircled Izzy as he continued to pick flowers from the pile and hand them out. Each person accepted the flower with a nod of thanks and a thoughtful quietude.

Izzy passed out the last flower, gave a nod of thanks and folded up the music stand, put the notebook in his satchel and called out to everyone that could hear to come back next week at the same time and he would be here to welcome them. The park emptied as darkness ushered in low key tones and edges softened into shadows and abstract shapes. Izzy backed up off the walkway and into the gray penumbra under the trees where he stood in silence with his eyes closed.

Back home Izzy paced the room before sitting down at the kitchen table, restless, tapping his fingers and looking all around his apartment. He was saturated with nervous energy and had a barrage of ideas whirring around inside his head. It was a dizzying and foreign sensation, but it delighted him and filled him with an enthusiasm he had never experienced before. He thought about next week and what he would do for his talk. Should he just show up and go with the mood that prevails at the time or put together a thought provoking, thematic speech written beforehand? He would start by writing down his thoughts each day and also copy several of the other messages that had washed ashore thus far. At the end of the week he would review all the material and decide whether or not to write out something of scope and breadth or use the notes as a starting point and let the direction follow from there.

Since the event in the park, the energy and reaction from the people who had experienced it was manifesting itself in numerous posts on Facebook. A couple of dozen people who were at the park the previous evening had posted images and descriptions of what had transpired. Soon hundreds of people were responding and adding their own insights and opinions about some of the social and philosophical notions that were expressed in the park that evening. Some voiced concern about the direction society was headed with regards to the Digital Age and social engineering on a global scale.

Are we losing the ability to think for ourselves and deferring such concerns to those assuming control of the dialogue via the internet and the constant collection of personal data? Have we grown impatient with controversy or opposing points of view, retreating into a world of one's own, devoid of reality, as a whole, and limited to one's subjective comfort zone?

Others stated their position with quite the opposite point of view, suggesting that we are on the threshold of a true awakening, spawned by access to massive stores of information not sullied by the spin of the mainstream media. Still others were confident that a spiritual revival was imminent, as all other facets of life and community had become empty and false. How are we to know what is real anymore? Is truth something that no longer requires confirmation? Is it simply synonymous with fact and beyond any desire for multiplicity and nuance?

The posts were building to a pitch, the like icon wearing to a dull blue gray and new chat groups popping up all over.

* * * * * * * * * *

The following week, Izzy entered the park and was astounded by the turnout and quite intimidated as well, to the point that he turned around before entering and stood across the street for a while, watching the crowd build, observing the patterns produced by the colors of people's clothing - blues and purples predominating, some bright and glowing, others soft and muted. Izzy preferred the saturated blues and purples and was especially keen on the variety of blue-violets that collected near the entrance to the park. He delighted in the spectacle of color swarming in and around the park. What a miracle color is he thought. He tried to imagine what the world would be like without color. Would it be gradations of black to white or would it be a monochrome, a blue marble with streaks of lights and darks swirling over and through it.

Why all this color though? Why does color mix and create a world of infinite hues? Why this chromotopia instead of just red, yellow and blue, devoid of all mixes and nuances in between? It all seems a bit overdone. Nature is magnanimous. It is not satisfied with being sufficient, it does not understand or have use for "just enough". Wherever it is capable of producing in bulk it does so.

The park was filling up and areas of congestion were developing in and around the entrance/exit points. Izzy figured he had better get over there and set up before he lost his nerve. He tried not to think of the crowd, he imagined it to be the same as it was the first time he came here to speak. This was his fourth talk and only a month had passed but it seemed much longer, much further back, deep into the past. In fact, it felt as though it had never happened, it was not real somehow. He was struck by the notion of how unreal things had been feeling lately. What did he do this past week, why does he not remember his day to day existence? Each day is a completely new experience with no recollection of past and no concern for the future, just a continual present. He was profoundly aware of his presence and the presence of everything around him from minute to minute. Sights and sounds coming and going, always new and always clear, without diffusion or distraction. A direct, unfiltered experience of continued renewal countered by a sense of separation, as though it was something outside of himself that was recording it all, as though he was the projectionist as well as the projector. It was hard to make any sense of it and he really did not need to make sense of it, he was merely taking it in and living inside and outside simultaneously. This is where time got skewed and dissolved almost immediately after each passing minute and was never

184

attached to an event ultimately.

Izzy found himself in the center of the park standing inside a water fountain, which had ceased functioning years ago, on top of a fake rock. He had not brought his notebook, or any other paraphernalia, just himself and his thoughts. He had a pretty good idea of how he wanted to start things off and where he wanted to go with it, his confidence bolstered by the massive crowd that was before him.

"Thank you all for coming here this evening. I see that our numbers have grown substantially since our last talk. *Truth spreads to all minds keen to its perceptions. This gives one the vision to see the true nature of things.* This was one of the longer messages to be transmitted across the ocean by bottle. It demonstrates the workings of a distinct mind, a vision unobscured by the veils of cultural and societal influence, a strength got by attentiveness and intuition. We can all attain this degree of clarity and truth if we can but step back and see around the edge to what is behind, destroy the mirrors we place in front of one another and see the infinite possibilities that lie within each of us."

A few people in the crowd cheered and chortled in accordance with what Izzy was saying. Some blurted out their own thoughts on the subject, punctuating them with yah's and woo's.

It was a lively scene, a real confluence of like- minded people, or at least like temperaments. Izzy let out a loud Wooo...and then someone else started a long, wavering, low pitched woooo that others joined in on and soon everyone was united in a series of long winded wooo's that sounded like wolves. The sounds were still flowing up and out of the park as Izzy exited and started back home. He was excited, high levels of adrenaline moving through him, yet relieved that it was over and that it went well.

Did it though?

He was beginning to wonder if the crowds were showing up at the park in order to attend a social event, like Facebook but in real time and in the flesh. They seemed to be coming there with their own agenda now, not so much to hear from him but to commune with friends, drink, get stoned and frolic amongst the masses. His initiative was losing ground to the energy generated by collective groups veering off in a variety of directions from spiritual concerns to political concerns to anarchy and individualism. He still regarded his actions as meaningful and he concluded that, in the end, the fact that so many people were gathering together, despite the reason, was a positive sign. If it turns out that his agenda becomes subordinate to the will of the people, then so be it. He did not want to give himself too much importance, it was more about the messages that came from the sea, of which he was the administer.

* * * * * * * * * *

Lying in bed Izzy was assaulted by a myriad of thoughts pertaining to his next talk. The dynamics were changing and he knew that he had but two options here. He could either direct the change or simply follow the change, wherever it may lead. It was not always in his nature to take control of things and initiate change, but this was a wholly new chapter in his life and passive deferment was not in the cards now. He still had a window, an opportunity to take control of the situation and direct the crowd back to a focused cause, steer it away from myopic, frivolous individualism. He thought of his friend Dado who could perhaps be an important help to him with respect to this. Dado was a DJ, a talented sound crafter and he was intrigued by the messages and what Izzy was doing in response to his, and all of the other, finds over the past ten months. Izzy realized the importance of atmosphere and mood to direct the flow of events, something to stir the emotions and lead people towards a collective awakening.

Dado could craft a series of ambient sounds - mood pieces, to augment his words and expand their effectiveness, inflate them to infinite proportions until the words and music merged into a powerful, complementary mind bend, capable of engaging the crowd as a whole. He got out of bed and sent Dado a text explaining his idea and asked for his input. If sustaining the dynamic. He hoped that Dado would have some good ideas to contribute relative to this.

Finishing the last of his coffee Izzy set out on his bike and headed down to the jetty for his meditation session. It was a bright but mild day and as he rode down the main road he was struck by the radiance of everything around him. He had grown accustomed to the heightened quality of all that he experienced lately but this morning seemed to offer something different, a level of awareness and pitch far stronger than before. This confirmed his feeling that everything was moving in the right direction, combining all his senses and intuitions into a lucid conceptualization of his purpose overall.

Sitting upon the rocks Izzy listened to the ocean and attuned himself to the rhythm, great swells heaving up and crashing onto the rocks, the resounding thud of water meeting the rocks with sudden impact, seething foam flowing over the rock surfaces, his senses aligned with all of it. Izzy was always greatly affected by the power of the Dado was interested, he should be prepared to get started immediately. In the morning, Izzy got up and while waiting for the coffee to brew, checked his phone. Dado had not responded yet.

Izzy did not want to decipher whether this was a good sign or not at this early stage, so he went back to the kitchen and prepared some toast.

Seated at the table, he planned-out the set up for the next talk, the functionless water fountain would be ideal. It provides a sanctioned space perfectly suited to a pedestal/podium, light and sound arrangement. It was "in the round" which allowed people to gather and surround him. Energy would be emanating out from the center of the fountain, rising up and expanding out and down the perimeter of the fountain – a continuous energy loop, a Torus that feeds back into itself. This, Izzy thought, was the quintessential visualization of his idea for connecting with the crowd and ocean, its ceaseless energy and enigmatic presence, especially in the evening when it seems to speak in hushed tones. He thought back on his journey along the coast and the tempest he endured on the evening before returning home.

There was a union that night, a coupling of mind and force, a thrashing that sparked the beginning of what Izzy now saw as an awakening and an empowerment. His meditations were deepening, he noticed a concentration of superlative focus. The world around him was in constant flux but this did not create chaos or uncertainty. It was balanced and natural, devoid of fear or anxiety. It was fluctuation, but it was informed fluctuation of an astute, insightful purpose.

Riding back home Izzy could not clear his mind of his new vision and he was eager to talk with Dado to discover, whether or not, he was ready for a challenge like this. How could he not be?

This was life affirming, something far beyond this common plane of existence. This was a calling to something already formed, teeming with energy and life, an organism that was born billions of years ago and now reaching supreme consciousness. The messages were a catalyst for bringing all of humanity together before we completely foul our nest and lead ourselves to extinction. This was nothing but a life or death struggle, a wakeup call to those ready to receive it.

Dado would surely see this and welcome the invitation to be part of it. Izzy was certain that there would be a text from Dado. He would check his phone as soon as he got back to the house. He never brought his phone with him when he went to the jetty, he loathed having any kind of distraction before or immediately after meditation.

When Izzy arrived home his phone was just then alerting him to an incoming message – it was Dado.

"yo dude, sounds frightening and delicious – let's talk"

Dado always spoke with a puzzling syntax but Izzy knew that this particular puzzle signaled acceptance. He was glad to have conformation from Dado and promptly called him back. The conversation lasted for over an hour and Dado already had some great ideas for music and presentation. He was confident that he could have it all arranged and ready for review by the end of the week, then finalized in time for the event. Izzy was very happy to hear this and arranged to meet with Dado on Friday. He hung up the phone and paced around the room, nervous energy and excitement folding into one another and leaving Izzy without control for the moment.

Eventually, he sat himself down and started to sketch out ideas for the talk on Sunday, examining a variety of words, phrases and gesticulations that could combine to form a dynamic, communicative experience overall. He spent the rest of the week practicing in front of the mirror, refining intonations and gestures so that people would be unremittingly focused on him at all times. Should he cut his hair, change his outfit or should he keep to a routine, signature style that does not interrupt the continuity. These were concerns that kept Izzy oscillating with indecision but by the end of the week he was resolved to keeping with the same clothes and hair, certain that this was the prudent thing to do. He was pleased with the ideas he had put together and felt that Sunday's event was going to set a new level for this whole endeavor.

He hoped to achieve a true breakthrough with this next talk and move into the realm of the "Great Communicator", a force to be acknowledged and celebrated. He considered the possibility that he was letting his ego get the best of him, but he had grappled with self- doubt for most of his adult life and now he was in the driver's seat and feeling a confidence that had been denied him in the past. He told himself that this wasn't about ego so much as about lost identity and misguided readings of himself. Finding the message in the bottle and grasping the implications of this find, and all that had transpired since, brought him to an awareness that had been dormant for far too long. Until now, his meditations were calming his inner noise but doing very little for his conscious wakefulness. The bottle message was a powerful revelation and not to be dealt with lightly.

Bringing Dado into the realm was another blessing. Having another person to share this experience with fed his courage and nourished his will. He could not help but sense the inevitability of the events that had transpired over the past ten months. He was seeing all of the pieces and how they fit, a quantum entangled "spooky action at a distance" that turned all events into one action.

Dado knocked on the door around 11am on Friday and Izzy swiftly opened it and gave Dado a hearty welcome. "Yo man, I've got some smooth synths to operate." Sounds great, said Izzy, coffee?

"Jazz", said Dado and started laying out some notes on the table. Some of the papers had rough sketches of the stage/fountain with ideas on how Dado wanted to utilize lighting and props. Izzy returned with the coffee and scanned the papers laying on the table. Dado pointed out some of the lighting arrangements that he had come up with and he and Izzy both worked on expanding the ideas to capitalize on the shape of the fountain as well as the opportunities the dark evening hours offered them. Dado mentioned that laser pens could be cool and really effective at bringing the crowd into the creation of the sound and light environment being formed. The word could go out to everyone through social media to bring laser pens, the greenish light variety, and Izzy could enact gestures for people to follow with the pens. Dado stressed the importance of an "interactive" environment, it was critical that people engage directly and form an integral part of the spectacle. Izzy was enamored with the idea and immediately sent out notices on Twitter and Facebook. He high five'd Dado and went to the kitchen to refill the coffee mugs.

* * * * * * * * * * *

Izzy was elated after Friday's meeting with Dado and spent

the next day shooting emails to him with and updates and confirmations. The laser pen idea was already taking off on social media, lots of posts demonstrating enthusiasm and listing shops and websites where the pens could be purchased. Most of what they needed was prepped and ready to go.

Sunday morning was beautiful, a clear sky, blazing with brilliant sunshine and seasoned with a smell of herbs from the neighbors garden in the back. Izzy never used the AC, he preferred the outside air, however warm or sultry it may be, to the controlled climate callousness of central air conditioning. He sat on the couch shining his shoes. This was an activity he truly loved, the transformation of the dull worn leather into a vibrant, shiny newness was wholly satisfying. This morning, shining his shoes felt like the wearing away of old ways of thinking and living, a polished clarity was taking hold. Seeing his reflection in the newly buffed shoe Izzy saw the distortion, caused by the contour of the shoe and creases of the leather, as a morphing of his being, a morphing of his former self into a new self, a self-molded by an absolute awareness of the "great chain of being". He thought about the breath that fogged the surface of the shoe before being buffed away. This was his old life, a clouded, vague existence lingering on the surface. He thought back to the storm and how the wind and rain had cleansed him, followed by the bright light of the moon that burnished his soul. Tonight, would be the culmination. This talk would be his deliverance from the cloud of unknowing, a transfiguration from flesh and blood to being and everythingness.

He lay down in his room, he would sleep for a couple of hours. Warm air swirled in from the open window and a faint humming, buzzing concoction lead him to sleep. Loud, simple music filled a large room crammed with people dancing, their movements random and lethargic. The music reduced to a quiet hum and then stopped altogether as did the people who were dancing; not because of some distraction but because time had stopped. Everything and everyone was frozen in time, a grim silence held, even the air was stilled. Then the door flew open and a beam of light, like a laser, streamed in hovering just above the floorboards, snaking in and out of the spaces between the dancers. As it passed, each person turned semi-transparent and a pattern formed within the contour of their body, a kind of cymatic pattern imprinted inside them that rendered visible their relative frequency. Magnificent geometric patterns creating complex symmetrical designs, each one unique as a snowflake, embodied each figure. The light beam then moved up toward the ceiling, formed a complete circle and then extinguished. Time resumed and dancing picked up where it had stopped, no one seemed to know that time had been suspended or that a beam of light had entered the room. Nothing was recorded in the minds of those who had been scanned by the light.

Izzy woke, sweating and completely still, his whole body was numb, it was like having an arm or leg "fall asleep" but it was his entire body. Every part of him was tingling and heavy, his arms and legs like rubber, his head an elastic ball. He lay there, quiet, his eyes the only movement, the room dark and cool. He was trying to remember where he was and whether it was early morning or night. The dream was strange and disturbing and aspects of it were slipping away by the second. He tried to hold on and remember everything as vividly as possible but it was no use. As feeling returned to his body the dream faded in direct relation, by the time he brought himself to a seated position, most of the details of the dream were gone. Izzy sat bemused, unable to do much other than stare into the blank darkness. Then the stoppage of time that had taken place in the dream streamed into his mind and he was fearful that many hours had transpired and he had missed the talk. Dado would surely have come by to get him if he had not shown up at the park, he thought, and that reassured him.

Yet, time still had to be confirmed and he attempted to stand up. It took a couple of tries, he was unstable but able to make it out to the kitchen. It was only seven o'clock, Izzy had two hours until the event. He got himself a glass of water and walked into the living room to look over the notes and the map for staging and props. He was satisfied with the scheme overall and eager to put it into action. He retrieved his clothes for the evening and laid them out on the couch, put the shined shoes below and a pair of socks on top of them, then went into the bathroom for a shower.

* * * * * * * * * *

The evening was warm with a slight sultriness to the air. The park was full of people, gathered in groups and moving in swarms. Dado was already there getting things set up so that Izzy could make any final adjustments when he arrived.

Energy and anticipation had been building in the park since the early afternoon, some had even slept overnight, hidden between bushes and rocks. The park had become something of a sensation now and many of the regulars had begun sprucing it up by planting flowers and edging the walkways, raking dry, hard, dirt and planting grass seed on the days that it rained. All of their efforts were coming to fruition and transforming the discreet, neglected nuisance into a pleasant, serene, vestige of nature. It had recently been listed on the city's map of popular sites with an artful blurb about the parks healing events that took place on a weekly basis by a "local spiritualist whose invocations have spurred new life into the park."

One could arrive from anywhere in the United States and easily find another person, or more likely, group of people from their state to connect with and attain introduction to others. Many areas of Europe and the East were represented in respectable numbers as well. It was a global microcosm, formed indiscriminately of like-minded, curious people. If one had arrived with little money and no familiarity with the city, this little park was the place to come for guidance and a friendly welcome. Those who had lived in the vicinity of the park for generations were astonished with its regeneration and reshaping in such a short time, by no will of the city or people of the neighborhood even. They were suspicious of the crowds that formed every Sunday but during most of the rest of the week it was a pleasurable spot to take a walk or sit and read.

Tonight, was Sunday though, so the park was in a very different state and as dusk approached the energy and buzz was growing exponentially like a culture of bacteria, no doubt a time elapsed view from a satellite would confirm the analogy. Izzy made a clandestine arrival by entering through a breech in the wrought iron gates at the back of the park across from an abandoned warehouse. Wearing a hoodie and looking more like an outsider than any of the people there for the event he weaved passed the crowds and joined up with Dado at the fountain.

"Hey man, fly me to the moon bro!"

"Hey Dado, what's up, how's everything going here?"

"All set and wait'in for lift off."

"Yeah, looks great man. No problem having enough juice for all of this right?"

"Enough for there and back bro."

"OK, get the smoke machine started and I'll let you know when to hit the first two lights."

"Douce"

Izzy opened his bag and pulled out some notes and a couple of laser pens. He stayed crouched down low in the fountain behind one of the larger of the fake rocks so that he was unseen by any of the park panoply. When everything was set, he pulled off his hoodie and motioned to Dado to hit the lights. The crowd gasped synchronously as a bluish mist rose- up out of the fountain. Dado eased in with a light ambient music. People in the crowd started flashing their laser pens, slicing through the smoke in all directions. Some of the crowd started chanting "Ultra, Ultra" in low, droning tones. Dado brought the volume up slowly and as he did Izzy climbed up on top of the fraud rock and spread out his arms, a laser pen in each hand pointed straight up towards the sky. As the music grew louder he brought his arms up to his head and crossed them behind, two beams of light shot out from behind his head and veered off into the rift of the night sky. The crowd flew into a riot of chants and cheers, lasers careening all through the park but centered mostly on the fountain and Izzy.

"We have light so as not to perish from the truth"

Woops and moans emanated from the center of the crowd, passing from one to another, until the sounds were repeated far to the perimeter. Izzy positioned his laser lights so that they pointed directly at his ears forcing great beams of light into the deep recesses of his head. The crowd followed suit and heads lit up all across the park.

"Light conquers darkness and allows us to see everything as it is – INFINITE"

Izzy took a long steady breath.

"Language will only create newer and stronger constraints – we must dismiss words and embrace the light of awareness" Izzy raised his arms and pointed his lasers towards the sky exhorting in a fever of energy....

"Hibba cha nubba ah khana khaneezer – mahah kanubb"

He continued to chant louder and more cryptic with each phrase. Dado brought the music up to a high and volatile pitch. The crowd was in a frenzy and lights were beaming throughout the sky, lighting up the low-lying clouds and creating a virtual Aurora Borealis. Dado had the smoke machine blowing full on and Izzy's voice was reverberating with massive distortion.

The smoke rendered him barely visible now and his voice unrecognizable as it penetrated the thin evening air. One final shrill erupted from Izzy and then his lights went out and all went quiet.

The crowd hushed momentarily and then exploded into howling and chanting. No one seemed to notice that Izzy had disappeared but all of the laser lights were directed towards the fountain, smoke still hovering above it and swirling slowly upwards. A few more cheers and woops were heard as the crowd dispersed and moved away from the fountain area.

Most of the people stayed inside the park, chatting and exchanging thoughts about the evening's event. Dado looked around for Izzy but after a couple of minutes, gave a shrug and started getting all the equipment together. I hope that fucker is not just going to leave me to deal with all of this shit, he thought. He decided to sit, have a smoke and wait. Izzy was probably hiding until the crowd dispersed so as not to be seen afterwards and spoil the performance by entering into real time and space. Dado presumed that Izzy would show up in the next fifteen or twenty minutes so hang and have a smoke, he figured, was the best plan.

Close to an hour had passed and Dado had finished packing up the equipment. He was surprised that Izzy had still not shown up. He lay his head back and fell asleep on the grass beside the fountain. The wind slid through the trees, rustling the leaves, insects buzzed around the fountain as faint sounds from outside the park carried over the cool night breeze.

A light mulchy smell was evident in the air. Fall was on the move and summer drifting off to the horizon. The park was empty, the sky full of stars and the Earth was spinning at 1000 miles per hour and careening about the sun at 67,000

www.ingramcontent.com/pod-product-compliance
Lightning Source LLC
Chambersburg PA
CBHW030646110726
47901CB00002B/591